The
Maple Sugar
Murders

Steve Sherman

The
Maple Sugar
Murders

Steve Sherman

Walker and Company
New York

First published in the United States of America in 1987 by the Walker Publishing Company, Inc.

Published simultaneously in Canada by
Thomas Allen & Son
Canada, Limited, Markham, Ontario

Library of Congress Cataloging-in-Publication Data

Sherman, Steve, 1938–
   The Maple sugar murders.

   I. Title.
PS3569.H4337M37   1987   813'.54   87-10400
ISBN 0-8027-5681-6

Printed in the United States of America

10 9 8 7 6 5 4 3 2 1

1

He loves to lie a-basking in the sun.
—W. S. Gilbert

AMOS REED BELLOWED into the telephone: "Hugh! Quit sitting on your head and going numb. Get yourself down here."

"If you want me to sweat for you, Amos, just say so."

"That's what I said. Get yourself down here and start stuffing wood."

"You're full of ersatz evil, Amos, you know that, don't you?"

"What're you talking about?"

"Remember when you were a kid?"

"No."

"You had some brothers and sisters you towered and powered over, didn't you, right? I know you did."

"I don't tower and power over *nothing*," Amos shouted. What a voice.

"You got them to snatch nickels from the kitchen change pot when mother wasn't looking or else, right? You know what I'm talking about."

"I got sap running and you talk nickels."

"You maneuvered those sweet, trusting, adoring little brothers and sisters to perform dirty work for you, and at such a thrifty price, Amos. Aren't you ashamed?"

"No."

"I knew some kid down the road where I grew up," Hugh said, "and he used to grab his sister's hand and

1

slap her own cheek with it. He got her smacked without really doing it himself, sort of. He got her to do it. That's ersatz evil, Amos. That's what I'm talking about."

"WHAT?"

"When you're growing up, this ersatz evil either grows you onto the Ten Most Wanted List or it stays at your level, Amos, a sort of tricky manipulation of friends and relatives. It all depends on a lucky mix of forces, not the least of which are the two seminal streams of Pythagorianism and Aristotelism, the yin and yang of Western civilization."

"WHAT?"

"Amos, we're devoted adherents to either the mysticism of number and the dark unknowable or the sunny adventure of knowing and understanding all there is to know and understand through our great human asset— reason. Of course, most of us end up like you."

"What're you *talking* about?"

"Well, anyway, we all take our turns, Amos, so that eases the humiliation of being managed by consent."

"I got a wrong number."

"I'll be right down."

Amos Reed made maple syrup, and he always got Hugh Quint to do dirty work for him. Hugh loved it. Amos sugared on a two-century-old family piece of land that bordered Chelsea Pond, a pre-Thoreauvian Walden. It was a pristine, granite-bottom paradise of Lyme water that had a Ganges spell on it, the kind of pond that made saints sinners.

This was summer thinking because snow was still covering the ground and the pond still iced over. When Hugh reached Amos's grove of maples, the sugarhouse was steaming like an old-time locomotive going nowhere. Steam billowed from the chimney in the center of the sugarhouse and, from a distance, the squat, hammer-

and-nail building looked on fire. Nothing was on fire except the roaring yellow-and-red logs under the evaporator.

Lyme was set deep in the isolating valleys where the white steeple church was seen piercing heaven just about from anywhere. The houses were rooted thick and old and kept shipshape. The footpaths were dirt-worn, not cemented. Main Street had a yellow line when someone got to painting it, and the businesses in town were the post office, the general store, the hardware store, the restaurant, the inn, and the school (the business of education). The realtors were always prominent, although people considered the real estate business a contradiction in terms. Their point was, how can you sell land and build houses when Lyme stood for *not* selling land and building houses?

"I saw you coming," Amos shouted, opening the wood-slat door. "You know Rita."

"Sure I do," Hugh said, nodding to Rita, who was hauling logs through the back door of the shed and stacking them next to the evaporator.

"One of my women," said Amos, sixty-eight years old by the calendar.

"Your only woman," she said, her quick eyes obliterating Amos's wink. Rita Dinsmore lived alone in an old farmhouse she had refurbished, and if Lyme had any tough-skinned woman of fifty or sixty (nobody really knew for sure how old she was) who was a nerve-racking environmental activist, she was it. Old jeans, scuffed boots, work gloves, blue plaid shirt, torn pocket, her hair cut like a lawn.

"She beat you here," Amos said, "and now she gets to stuff wood."

"Women get the best work," she said, opening the stove door and throwing two logs inside like squash seeds. "That's what Benj says, too."

"Benj who?" Amos growled, scowling at the female.

Rita turned over a galvanized pail, stood on it, and reached for the bare light bulb.

"What're you doing up there?" Amos shouted.

"I'm changing the bulb. I can hear it's going. You want to change it at night in the dark?"

"I know you're changing the bulb. On that PAIL?"

Rita looked at her feet.

"You want to FALL IN THERE?"

"I guess you're right," she said, stepping down.

"Sure I'm right."

"I thought you were worried about your pail."

"Sure I'm worried about my pail."

She and Hugh grinned, while Amos whirled his arms to say get on with it and don't get mushy.

The fire was hell-blazing red, too hot for the sap in the flatbed evaporator above, so Rita used fresh logs to soften the heat. That way the sap wouldn't burn. The heat and the boiling sap, the steam rolling up and out, the pipes and filters and funnels and jugs—they jammed the tight sugarhouse for the ancient ritual. The marly odor of rich maple permeated the shed, and that was what made it all sumptuously seductive, working hard for the sweet, earthly smell, the thick, emulsive tree sugar. Hugh loved the stuff.

"Well, am I going to get to test it or not?"

"Test it?" Amos shouted. "You haven't *worked*. What do you mean test it?"

"Another hoarding Yankee. I need a sip. How do I know if it's worth working for?"

"Give the man a sip, Amos," Rita said, grinning, leaning against the slab-wood wall. "He's going into convulsions."

"It's a sip, now. I thought it was a test. Sure, I'll give him a sip soon as we get more sap. Come on."

There they went out the door, leaving Rita to shake her

head and roll her eyes as she tossed in another log below the bubbling sap. She was the fire-watcher, as someone must be at all times, while Hugh and Amos trudged through the snow to the baby tractor and skidder. Amos started it up, Hugh jumped on the skidder, and together they crawled over the white ground through the trees.

"Couldn't sugar without her," Amos said, shouting about as close to an extravagant compliment as he could muster, except that he added: "You can't do this alone, you know. She's some woman, and in my day, well . . ."

"Well, what?"

"You know what I'm talking about."

"You talking about the birds and bees, Amos?"

"Benj," he said, spitting out the B-for-bastard word, changing the subject fast. "You heard her back there. 'That's what Benj says, too,' she says. She's getting back at me, that's all. She does that. Getting back at me. Trying to make me something."

"Trying to make you what?"

Amos turned a bulldog face to Hugh.

They hiked on up the half-swampy snow.

Finally, Amos said it: "She's getting back at me," he said, letting Hugh know that no woman had *him* in tow, " 'cause I told her I found out Benj is dying of cancer like his brother. Told her I found out that Benj is right now making a secret deal with a developer for his own land. Selling out. Going to live high on the hog while he can because, he says to me, we all die of cancer anyway. Irritates her."

"Is that true, Amos?"

He turned and grinned.

"So you're getting back at her."

"She's getting back at *me!"*

"Do you have to irritate her, Amos? She's always over at your place, you know, not Benj's."

"She's a woman, ain't she?"

Amos never went all modern. Most of his sugaring was done with the new blue plastic tubing that linked one tree with another so the sap flowed continuously down the line and straight into 50-gallon barrels at the bottom of the hill. That way he could pump out the barrels into a holding tank on the skidder, tractor it to the sugarhouse, and then pump the sap high into a feed tank that led by gravity to the evaporator. Commercial outfits had it all worked out like that on a huge scale. Amos tapped 500 trees, not too many, enough to boil up 150 gallons or so, depending how good the season was. For old times' sake, he kept 50 trees in one corner of the orchard for pails, the postcard way. He kept the tractor away, too. Matter of principle. That meant snowshoeing to the pail section when it was deep snow cover, which now it wasn't.

"You ain't sweating, are you?"

"This is play, Amos. I'm having fun."

"Looks painful on you."

"Naw," Hugh said, aching.

"Come on. I'll show you something."

Amos led the way up the hill to the crest and the end of his property. Hugh was breathing hard, all right, but old Amos kept trudging on his husky legs, his thick, green wool pants moving like clockwork. He wore red suspenders in winter, red plaid shirt over a green, high-neck shirt underneath, thick black and red wool overjacket, and a billed, checkered wool cap. They hiked through the woods with sun-stealing brush cleared away, sugarless birches cut out, the whole red maple lot looking like a garden. That was how Amos Reed made syrup.

They stopped at the crest, and Amos spread his hand toward the next sugar orchard. He said out the side of his mouth, "Look at that. Wonder Benj gets a gallon out of it. See that line sagging there? Probably kinked up.

Probably not even running. The ol' boot is probably at home, snoozing. Thinks it's going to boil up itself."

"Well now, Amos, no hard feelings between you two, are there?"

"Hard feelings?" he said, turning to Hugh, eyes puzzled (what an actor!). "No hard work between us is what it is. I do the work, he does the 'no,' if you get my drift."

Hugh grinned to make sure he wasn't siding too much with Benj. Anyone who didn't know the steely air between Amos Reed and Benj Carver hadn't lived in Lyme two weeks. "I get your drift, and maybe you make a little better syrup than Benj, but—"

"Little better? Take a look at that lot. Brush all over. Can't move your toe. Line sagging like that. Probably missing half of what the trees are giving. Nope, Benj just ain't *got* it, that's all. Last time I spotted him out here he was gathering sap and spilling half of it. Soaked right up. Gone. Trying to get it primed in the ground for next year, I guess. You know what I mean?"

"Right, Amos."

"Well, the ol' boot's always been that way, Benj has. Jealous. Like the time I got one hundred eighty-five gallons and he's working up a sweat getting fifty, maybe. I don't think he got that much that year. Feel sorry for the aging man. He's jealous. He hates me for keeping this place. I tell him it's settled. I keep telling him that. I got this land because his father, he's in the ground back there in town, his father didn't deal right with my father. And that's the bottom of it." Father meant forefather.

"It's an old feud."

"No feud at all. Not by me. I just wish he knew a thing or two." Amos stopped and studied Hugh with a sly eye. "Something else been going on lately. You don't know these things, you traveling here and there in the big cities and all."

"What's going on?"

"Lots of pressure on me lately. Lots of pressure. Benj wants my land here, always did. He goes too far, too. I been seeing some of my buckets empty. You get my drift?"

"I'm not sure, Amos."

"You do all right. I come around collecting and I see these buckets of mine empty. Now, no squirrel is going to drink up all these buckets. And I sure didn't collect them. Don't you think I know that much?"

"Could be anything. Deer, maybe."

"Yeah, big city people'd say that. Next thing Benj'll say it was some great grizzly come strolling through from Alaska and had himself a drink or two. Nope. It's Benj trying to get back at me. I even had one of my lines cut. The sap dripped half a day right out before I spotted it. Lost that sap. Costs me money, you know."

Hugh nodded sympathy.

"He's trying to give me havoc. He wants my lot so he can work all these trees himself, keep it all himself. What he don't know is that it takes work, and he's the 'no' part of the no work."

"I heard that squirrels chew up the plastic."

"They do and I catch them at it, too. And he tried to make it look like squirrels, but what do you think, I don't know what squirrel teeth do? Nope. Even Davy Tefler been after me a few times. He's been out here at the sugarhouse even. Calls me on the telephone at home. He says if I want to sell it, let him know. He'll get me a good price."

"Can't blame him for trying."

"Why not?"

"Well, I don't know, Amos. You got me there."

"Sure I do."

He stepped off and Hugh followed him along the ridge. He was heading back to the blue-tube section of his orchard and shouting about this and that when he stopped dead in his tracks. He peered down the slope into Benj's orchard. "Can't tell for sure," he said, shaking his head, "but I think the ol' boot is doing what comes naturally again. Look at him, snoozing on the job."

Hugh couldn't locate him.

"There. On the other side of them birches. Those should've been cut out ten years ago. He's sitting down there, thinking the trees are doing the work when he should be." Amos shouted into the thick trees that sponged in the sound, "Hey, Benj! You playing solitaire or something?"

Finally, Hugh saw him in the distance. To an eye not attuned to every tree trunk of any thickness, to every shadowy boulder and seedling, as Amos was around there, it took time. Benj was sitting against a maple all right, half hidden by the intervening trees, puffed up in a green winter parka.

"Hey, Benj!" Amos shouted. "You playing Rip Van Winkle?"

No response. Amos studied the scene, the detached woodsman, journeyman, man-of-outdoors.

"What's he doing?"

"You don't sleep in the snow," he shouted. "Come on."

He ran down the far side of the crest into Benj's orchard. Hugh followed, stumbling in the misleading snowdrifts the wind had banked against oaks and granite. He kept glancing at Benj in the distance, and trying to keep up with Amos.

Amos's quick movements showed alarm. He was jumping through the snow, weaving in and out the trees, his arms and legs working with the special adrenal yearning to operate efficiently because something extraordinary was happening: You don't sleep in the snow.

With white breath spurting out their mouths, Hugh and Amos ran up to the man leaning slumped against the tree trunk, his legs stretched out, his boots angled outward. The men stood staring down, wordless. It wasn't Benj. It was Davy Tefler. Ashen, bluish, cold bluish. His arms spread to his side, his brown-gloved fingers curled like winter oak leaves. His body curved in a misshapen L and sagged to the left. It wasn't going to fall to the ground because blue plastic tubing was wrapped twice around his neck and then around the circumference of the maple trunk again and again. Tight.

2

Revenge his foul and most unnatural murder.
—Shakespeare

AMOS CAME BY Hugh's place two days later. He stomped the slush off his Maine boots, glanced around the room, and sat in a corduroy chair. He belonged in the woods; he was out of sorts. With a tight, thin mouth, he said, "Benj been to see you about this?" Lips cracking his leathery face, diluted blue eyes unwavering.

"No, he hasn't, Amos."

"He will."

"Oh?"

He nodded like a preacher in a pulpit. "The Chief is accusing me."

"Now, Amos, he took a statement from you, that's all. That's his job, he has to cover himself. We were the first ones there. He took one from me, too, you know."

"Makes no difference. He's accusing me, and so's Benj, the old beat-up dodo bird."

"Benj isn't accusing you. He's just—"

"How do you know? You said he ain't been up here."

"That's right. I'm just saying that—"

"He'll be up here, only I want you to get to him first. You go down and talk to him first."

"Amos, the Chief'll take care of it."

"The Chief couldn't find his foot in a shoe."

"Well, this isn't exactly your computer-based metropolitan precinct."

"They fired you off the Boston police, didn't they? Big detective."

"I quit."

"Can't stick with nothing. Too educated, I guess."

"We all have our problems."

"Now you're a big deal private eye, right?"

"Investigator, Amos. Private detective. Yes, I've got a license."

"Couldn't do nothing else, I guess. Got to do something."

"Right, Amos."

"Anybody can get a license around here. Nothing to that."

"Just pay your hundred dollars and don't rob banks."

"Thought so. Don't give you any more rights than me, being a private whatever. Just the right to charge money."

"Right, Amos."

"Thought so." He glanced around the cottage. "How come you live in this shack? You probably got more money in your wallet right now than the town gives the Chief all year. You musta been a real rejection for your people to kick you up here. 'Course, I never trusted those Back Bay Brahmin high-noses anyhow, whichever way you look at them. Besides, they're too far away to amount to anything, down there with all them street lights and parking meters. Yeah, your people musta figured you could do *something,* someplace, so it might as well be up here in the woods, reading books, because they musta figured you couldn't do *nothing* down there, with all that money to boot. Ha."

Hugh stared at the bellowing-voiced clump of a man.

"Yeah, Harvard. Reading this and that. Words. GREEKS. You trying to be some kind of *philosopher* or something, only you run out and do this and that and who knows what. I know phi*los*ophers who can't wash a dish.

Private detective, huh? Philosopher *drop-out*, sounds to me. You know how to wash a dish?"

"Are you through, Amos?"

Amos stood up like an explosion; one never questioned the source of his strength. " 'Course, I guess you figure I can't afford you, that's what you're figuring. Money doesn't do nothing for friends and acquaintances. I know about it." He stepped to the door. " 'Course, you didn't know Davy Tefler, did you? So that's the difference. I didn't like him much either, always selling land instead of improving it. Wouldn't kill him, though." He turned the doorknob.

"Now, Amos, don't go off in a brood," Hugh said, standing up.

"Why not?"

"Because."

"That ain't no reason. And you read books. You couldn't bother calling Boston for an old acquaintance about what price they're selling syrup down there let alone saving him from the electric chair or hanging. They hang here, you know. Trying to change it to lethal injection, but what's the difference?"

Hugh smiled, feeling suckered by a pro. "I'll check around, Amos."

Amos stopped turning the knob. "You check Benj, only keep in mind what he thinks of me."

Hugh called Proctor Hammond, his answerman, his test-tube know-it-all, the man who said to anyone, even old-friend Hugh, on lifting the receiver: "Speak."

"Quint."

"Not again. I'm busy."

"You're always busy, Proctor. What's it this time? Bubbling up some pencil lead to see how much gold you get out of it?" Hugh stretched his long track-and-field legs across the pine plank table with copies of *The*

Humanist and *Crime Today* on top. He smiled at the inevitable to come.

"Big comedian. You think alchemy is a joke because you live like Tarzan in the trees up there. Civilization is cities. Civilization is Boston. It's city people who know that alchemy is what's going on today. They're changing elements. Laugh, you ignorant twig. In the old days they purified lead to get gold. Now they're purifying silicon to get electricity out of sand. Nobody knows anything. Seven hours and eight minutes every day every week every month every year Americans have the TV on. No wonder ignorance reigns."

Hugh listened to Proctor's high, scratchy voice rapid-fire through the phone. He imagined the owl-eyed misfit pacing back and forth in his office full of tornado debris. The man was mad for facts and lived to tell the world to shove it, like an almanac gone berserk. He was an archivist. Perfect. Only someplace like Boston University could file this special creature upstairs in the Mugar Memorial Library, Special Collections, and computerize him a check for his meat and drink. He was a sort of poodle with a brain; he irritated everybody.

"Judas, Proctor, you're going to be rich with all that gold. You want me to send you some pencils?"

"Stick the pencils in your lapel, Hugh."

"So you're not alchemizing after all."

"You're taking my time."

"Dissecting ant legs again?"

"Baseballs."

"Judas, Proctor."

"A billion dollar business and nobody knows a thing about them. I cut one in half and measured it."

"Measurement is all, Proctor."

"I haven't measured a syllogism yet, Hugh Quint. Syllogisms don't weigh much with me. No length, no width."

"Therefore, they don't exist."

"Baseballs you can weigh," Proctor said, ignoring Hugh's jab, "so I cut one. It's got a cork center one and three-eighths inches in diameter. Then three layers of wool, polyester, and cotton yarns. The first layer makes the ball two and one-half inches in diameter, the second layer three and three-quarters thick. Then the finish layer smooths it. Two hundred layers total, plus or minus five."

"Human error."

"Indulge yourself, twig, while you got the chance. After they're wound up, they're dipped in latex glue. Then two horsehide figure eights are cut for the cover. Horsehide is tougher than cowhide. Millions of baseballs are used every year, and nobody knows a goddamn whit about them. The world's stupid. The covers are intriguing. No machine has ever been invented to sew on covers right. They're sewn on by hand, it takes great skill. Not in this country. Cheap slave labor in Haiti does it."

"You're a wealth, Proctor, a real wealth."

"Laugh all you want, stone wall in the snowy woods. Good-bye."

"How much is syrup selling for down there?"

"Seven-fifty a quart. Twenty-nine fifty a gallon on Newbury Street. It has to be good. No paraformaldehyde tablets in the tap holes to get the sap flowing."

"It's good, and he doesn't use the tablets."

"Whoever he is."

"Oh, just a murder suspect," Hugh said and hung up, laughing at Proctor Hammond ravaged by curiosity.

Benj Carver didn't shave much. Now and then. His house was a cabin waiting for new thick brown paint, some window washing, someone to hammer the warping clapboards that rusted nails let loose. He kept an old pot-belly woodstove, just in case, outside by a pile of twisted and ripped rattan chairs he had collected from the dump. His new stove was twenty years old. The front seat from a Ford sedan had stuffing erupting from the back, but it was good for sitting in the summer outside when the black flies were long gone and July mosquitoes were fading. Benj preferred the heave-to effect for his woodpile. Stacking meant city slickers.

"I heard you coming," he said, opening the door as Hugh approached the slouchy house.

"Benj, how are you?"

Benj Carver was in the upper decades, like Amos Reed. He was a loner, like Amos, and he was from an old rooted family line, like Amos. That was the trouble. Mirror images tended to ricochet too much, emphasize the warts. Cancel each other out. Hugh knew the syndrome, but Amos and Benj maybe didn't.

To hear Benj tell it, Amos's family line forged the papers that deeded the Reed land—by the shore—when all along the land was in Carver hands for ten years before the Reeds came to town. The Reeds were a horde of conniving hoodlums who stacked the town office with cronies, had the cronies impose thieving tax fines that forced the Carvers to move off, and forged those early papers. Some Carver shot some Reed back then, and for good reason, so naturally the Reeds were out for revenge sooner or later. The Reeds came up from some stucco town in Massachusetts someplace, of course, but the Carvers moved over from real Vermont country. That was the difference.

The reason that no Reed had killed a Carver in revenge yet, so far anyway, was because the Reeds already had the shore land on Chelsea Pond. But no Carver forgot that forgery, and if Amos thought some Carver was going to shoot another Reed sometime soon, well, let him. Anyway, that land-thieving business wasn't settled yet.

16

Besides, everybody knew that Amos Reed was a wood-stacking slicker come up to claim he was from one of the original settling families of Lyme. Lies. The Reeds claimed they had a name change back when sheep were raised and the mill was going, but the Carvers knew better because the Carvers were here first. When you're here first, you're seeing who comes after. No records showed anybody changing names. It was just stealing the land. Carvers didn't forget.

"Now this happens," Benj said, sunk in an elephant-thick green armchair, the high back smudged from years with his greasy hair. The skirting was half-torn and tilted on the floor. "He near murdered me in revenge, didn't he?"

"You think that?"

"I know it. It was on my land, wasn't it? Amos Reed'll do anything. He gets his ideas from Massachusetts."

Hugh twisted his mouth to keep from grinning. He had patrician bones, the lean imperialism of favored blood, the blue eyes and sandy hair of latter-day Caesarism. He saw the daggers of forked tongues flickering out Benj's eyes, the double-duty thrusts at Amos and the visiting Augustus. Massachusetts was full of blood-dripping revolutionists in the 1700s. What was true then was true today. Now was not the time for Hugh to high-chin it. "It was Davy Tefler, Benj."

"It was on my land."

"But it was Davy Tefler, and Amos was with me when we found him."

"It was a trick. He's getting back. It coulda been me strangled there on my own land. If it wasn't Amos, who was it?"

"They're trying to find out."

"You're trying."

"Benj," Hugh said, looking straight into the man's

creased pumpkin face with the clamped umbrella-line mouth, the scowling eyebrows, the inky eyes, "I live here, too."

"Not for long."

Hugh shook his head. "No, not for long, but I knew Davy."

"Davy was pestering me," Benj said. "Sell my land? Never. I'll get the Reed patch when old Amos kicks it. You'll see. Carvers outlive the Reeds. Living like a city slicker kills people early."

"Davy wanted Amos to sell, so you're not the only one. He wasn't picking on you, Benj."

"I told the Chief all I know. I told him Amos did it."

"Come on, Benj."

"Come on where?"

Hugh smiled. "You sound like Amos."

"I sound like Amos because he sounds like me. That's where it stops. He killed Davy to blame it on me. Strangled him right here on my own land. He wanted to kill me, get back, but he missed me. Got another plan. He wants to blame me for the killing to get me out of the way."

"What for?"

"To get my land, what do you think?"

"He liked Davy."

"Nobody liked Davy."

"Well, I don't know, Benj."

"I do. Nobody likes people selling land and ruining it. You look at that Amos doing what he did to that land, that land he stole back there forging the deed and all that. He got that land next to the pond, thieved it, and then them Reeds start sugaring like they were in downtown New York. Making it into Central Park. You stroll through it like Central Park. What do they know in Central Park? Nothing."

Hugh shrugged: Take no sides.

"Best piece of stolen land around here, best pond anywhere, and what does he do? He clips it. Next he's going to plant tomatoes in it and little pansies."

"He's been sugaring it a long time, Benj."

"You don't prune paradise."

Hugh puckered and nodded, throttled by the stupendous words coming from the grizzled, hump-shouldered man glowering across the braided throw rug undoubtedly snatched from the town dump before it was set to fire.

"Land's wild," Benj said, "natural. You keep land the way it is and let it be. Take some sugar, take some logs. You don't manicure it like Amos Reed and his horde, do you?"

"Probably not."

"Here's what you ask Amos Reed. You ask the son-of-a-bitch if he didn't kill Davy, why is he blaming me?"

"Is he?"

"Sure he is. He thinks because Davy was strangled right here on my own land, right with my own tubing, that I did it. That's the kind of horde you're dealing with."

"Benj, why don't you ask him yourself? It might be a good time to start talking again, you two."

Benj Carver dropped his head another inch, angling his dark eyes deeper beneath his bushy eyebrows. He stared, flabbergasted, at Hugh, totally bewildered, the words failing his sliver-thin mouth. Finally: "I don't talk to stranglers."

3

With many a foul and midnight murder fed.
—Thomas Gray

TWO DAYS LATER, a Saturday, Hugh returned to Benj's place to find out what exactly Davy Tefler had been trying to brew up with Benj. Was Tefler twisting arms on both Amos and Benj? Pitting one against the other?

The ground was the usual soggy sugaring March rendition—cold nights and hot days. It made the sap flow. If you got outside early enough, your boots hit hard sod and crusty snow; you got out late and the sun melted you in. Hugh shouldn't have waited so long.

He headed for the sugarhouse with flabby steam climbing out the chimney pipe. Maybe ol' Benj was just starting up. Maybe it was just casual Benj holding back on burning too much wood, being the kind he was.

Then Hugh caught the smear of a shadow out the corner of his eye. It was pure movement in the trees on the hill, nothing else, too far away to distinguish it, a quick blur and gone.

First thought: a deer. But on a Saturday afternoon when weekend people filtered into town, the comings and goings eliminated that possibility. No, it was a man-made shadow in a hurry.

It wasn't Benj, not running away on his own property, not tired, pokey Benj. And it was too far away to run after it. Why do that anyway? Hugh was halfway up the tangled path that led to the Carver sugarhouse with the steam limping out the chimney.

"Benj?"

He creaked open the door and kept himself at arms length against the silence that shouldn't inhabit a sugarhouse in sap season. "Benj?"

Instinct did it. Hugh pressed himself against the outside wall as he eased the door wider. This time the shadow he saw slip over the rise, the unnatural blur disappearing into the brush and thickets that Benj refused to trim, flashed through his mind.

"Judas."

Benj Carver lay face down in the boiling sap.

Hugh whirled toward the shadow. Useless. Too far gone. Headed out of sight toward the Perley place.

He turned back to Benj and knew while he stepped toward the evaporator that the old, grizzled codger was through. The sap was still steaming, the temperature dropping to simmer, the hard boiling bubbles finished. The man's face and hands were half submerged, and where the boiling sap had subsided the skin was scorched and burst, seared like branding irons, split. Ugly.

The sugarhouse was a mess. Partly it was Benj's way. Hugh saw a bench on its side; buckets and jugs were scattered around, probably from a struggle, but who could really tell? Some filter funnels and cloth lay on the floor; they shouldn't be there. Hammers and bow saws and axes were strewn about. Logs were kicked out of symmetry, but that was all natural to Benj.

Benj's legs floated in a V, his heavy booted feet anchored deeper than the rest, but not entirely, because the sap was dense and supporting. The sap had bubbled up and thickened over the back of his pants and shirt. Hugh wanted to grab Benj and yank him out of the sap, but he'd burn his own skin off. What was the point?

He stared at the grotesqueness. The sap was cooling, the fire underneath the evaporator dying. He looked over the room again: What was Benj's mess, what wasn't?

He stepped outside, suddenly vulnerable in the silence, the ugliness behind him. The high sun was melting the snow. The ground at the door and the woodpile was stamped helter-skelter with Benj's footprints. Hugh looked to the rise—and started to run through the slush.

He cut diagonally through the brush, slipping in the mush. He found the tracks.

Big tracks. Headed to the rise. Clear and deep. Fresh.

The edges of the bootmarks were clean and sharp in the wet snow, cut out like a paper punch. But they wouldn't last. He sprinted after them, matching the running leaps to the rise. The snow was melting fast. Already around the base of the boulders it had melted away from the heat of the sun that the granite radiated. Some of the dirty, hard-packed snow around the big maples was rotted through like fungus.

Hugh reached the rise and stopped. No movement in sight. Nothing out of place. Nothing but dark trunks, gray boulders, patches of mud. Silence. The white and umber woods. The tracks marked the snow down the rise and headed toward the gravel road that connected the entrances to the Perley, Carver, and Reed places.

Patience. Get the facts. Details. He studied one of the bootprints and bent down to measure it with his outstretched hands. From thumb to little finger Hugh cleared nine inches. The print extended three more inches. This was a big man. Allowing for the usual oversize of a boot, he was probably size eleven, maybe twelve. It was impossible to tell from a running print, but traces of grooves at the toe meant a Maine boot, leather on top, rubber on bottom. Standard stuff for mud season. Everyone wore them. Impossible to trace.

He stood up and ran down the rise, following the prints

in a straight line to the road. He slipped and recovered before stumbling to the ground. His breath was frosting; he was making the only noise. He didn't see any prints that slipped as he did.

When he reached the road, his thighs ached. Worse than running the 880 dash.

The tracks leaped the drainage gulley and imprinted deep in the wheel section of the gravel-and-sand road, almost squishy. Hugh leaped across and sank, too. And stopped. The tracks headed down the road. The snow was gone from the road, driven over and melted away; no trees blocked the sunlight.

He ran down the middle of the road, still matching the running prints egging him on. Then he lost them. The road turned dry as a bone. Full of packed gravel. He stopped. Nothing showed on the side or in the snow along the edge of the woods. He ran on, and the thick, deep tracks appeared again in the next spongy section of sand.

It was clear that the tracks were headed toward the connecting road to town.

When Hugh reached the asphalt, he ran a few yards to follow the sandy remains that shook off the boots. Then the tracks disappeared. He stopped and looked uselessly back and forth, up and down. Forget it. Waste of time. Impossible.

It was closer to circle around to the gravel road to Amos's place than to town, so Hugh trotted back. Benj had no telephone and the Perleys were still down on the Cape. He had to get the Chief.

Amos was driving the tractor and skidder down the slope to his sugarhouse as Hugh trotted down the entrance road and the path past the house. Amos cut off the engine and cursed the noise that it left behind. Rita opened the sugarhouse door.

"You know how to tell big city people around here," Amos shouted. "They jog. Running on their brains is what they do." He climbed down and thumbed back his fist at the holding tank of fresh sap. "Full," he told Rita.

"Just in time," Rita called to Hugh. "You can stuff wood."

Then they stared at Hugh breathing hard, straight-faced, getting no reaction from him. "You look painful," Amos said.

"Something's happened."

"Something always does," Amos said, realizing too late that Hugh was serious.

"What's the matter?" Rita said, removing her leather work gloves, pulling them off finger by finger.

"Benj's dead."

They froze wide-eyed. Struck dumb. Unbelieving.

Hugh nodded. "Can I use your phone? I better call the Chief."

"Benj?" Amos said, his eyes fixed on Hugh's.

"Hugh, what happened?" Rita said, spreading her hands, her gloves stuffed in her jeans back pocket.

"Where is he?" Amos shouted. "What do you mean? DEAD?"

"I have to use your phone, Amos. He's over at the sugarhouse."

Amos turned and marched toward Benj's lot.

"Amos, wait a minute," Hugh called. "Let me call the Chief first. I better go with you."

Amos kept on.

"Amos!" Rita shouted. "Wait a minute. We'll all go. It's better, all right?"

That worked. He turned around and rooted his feet in place, challenging Hugh to get the goddam phone call called and get on with it.

Rita went inside the sugarhouse and closed down the fire under the evaporator, while Hugh hurried inside

24

Amos's house and called Chief Atkins. Then the three of them plodded through the spring slush and mud, up and over the rises to Benj Carver's place, marching wordlessly through the brush and fallen white birch limbs and rotting trunks.

Hugh stopped them at the door of Benj's sugarhouse. "It's ugly," he said.

"He lived ugly," Amos said. "What's the difference?"

To soften it, Hugh said, "You want to wait for the Chief?"

"The Chief'll take all weekend to find this place," Amos said. "Probably has to send to Washington, D.C. for a map."

Hugh glanced at Rita. When she shrugged, he twisted the knob and opened the door.

They walked in and stared a minute at Benj Carver floating in the sap.

Finally, Amos said, "Jesus Christ, the ol' boot ruined his last batch of syrup."

"Amos!"

Then Rita caught Hugh's eye, and the shock turned to a laugh.

"Well, didn't he?" Amos shouted.

"Amos," she said, "he can't help being the way he is."

"WAS."

She turned to Hugh. "This is awful. Awful. What happened?"

Before Hugh could say anything, Amos shouted, "He jumped in."

"Come on, Amos."

"Come on where?"

"He was pushed," Hugh said.

"Look at him," Amos said, dismissing the sticky, gummy body with a jerk of his finger. "Snoozing to the very end."

"Why that?" Rita asked, ignoring Amos. "He could have slipped. Maybe he was on this bench or something, trying to fix something. I don't know. Maybe trying to tighten that valve up there. I do that, and I shouldn't."

"Maybe. Maybe somebody pushed him into it when he was up there. I don't think it was an accident, Rita."

She waited, and so did Amos.

"I came up to see him, talk to him. Like you said, Amos. I saw some fresh tracks. I think I just missed whoever it was. There was nothing to do for Benj, so I followed those tracks. They went down near Perley's place."

"HA!" Amos shouted. "I never trusted them Cape Cod crud coming up here on weekends, slumming in here like interest on a bank loan. What'd I tell you? I told you about them, didn't I? Benj *hated* 'em and they hated Benj. That's who did it, huh?"

Hugh waited for Amos Reed's head to stop bobbing the accusation. "They didn't go down to the Perley house, Amos. I followed them down to the road, then down to Route 148."

"So what?"

"So the Perleys aren't up here yet."

"They are," Rita said.

"See!" Amos said.

"Well, the tracks disappeared," Hugh said, filling the gap, saying something.

"It has to do with Davy Tefler, doesn't it?" Rita said.

"Benj sold syrup to the Perleys for three dollars more than in town, and that's why they hate him. Because *he* hates them. Clipped them. I woulda done it, too, only he beat me to it. He was always doing that, cheating me. Now look at him. Soaking up his own syrup. He'd do anything to get back at that Perley crowd, coming up here and driving a Cadillac next to his woods. So this is

26

what he did, Benj. He jumped in and blamed it on the Perleys. Pretty smart for a Carver."

Chief Atkins drove up in his blue-and-white. He walked in and nodded to the three of them standing at the vat. He stared at the floating corpse. "Jesus."

Hugh recounted the scene for the Chief, who looked at him with his soulful grey eyes above his jowly cheeks, his bulbous nose. No Lyme Chief headed for Florida retirement wanted two murders in one week. Hugh knew Atkins enough, saw enough. The fifteen-year-old pot-belly on the fifty-eight-year-old frame. The white under-shirt glaring through the stretched button at his holster buckle and belly button. The sallow look of his cruiser-shielded skin. A lifetime in the shade. Chief Atkins was putting in time.

"I'll get the rescue boys up here," he managed, "and get him out of there." He went to the cruiser, radioed in, and strolled back.

"Hugh here says those tracks went to the Perley place," Amos told the Chief. "What do you think?"

"We'll talk about it later," the Chief said.

"Why not now?"

"In my office, Amos."

"That's an office?"

The Chief nodded, but it was a sleepy-eyed, pacifist defense against the usual Amos Reed assault.

"What about the tracks?" Amos shouted.

"I'll look at them."

"You *ran* over them. Your cruiser squished them right out. Then the rescue truck comes and squishes them out, too. The truck's doing it right now," Amos shouted. "RIGHT NOW."

When the red-and-white rescue truck arrived with flashing lights, the crowd jammed into the sugarhouse and again cursed the sight of Benj Carver floating in the vat. Amos shouted orders. The Chief told the rescue squad to get the body out before it got stuck there. The squad debated how to do it. Hugh said to slip a belt loop around the body and pulley it out.

Someone came maneuvering his way through the gaggle of men watching, mesmerized. It was Henry Perley. He cursed the sight and asked the Chief what was happening. He'd seen the Chief's car drive down the road, then the rescue truck, then all these people. What happened to Benj Carver?

The Chief said, "You can see what happened. I'll talk to you about it later. We have to clear him out of here."

"Damn thing to happen," Perley said. "Right next door. And Tefler strangled. What's going on around here?"

Perley stepped to the side when the rescue squad, grunting and groaning and shouting at each other, pulleyed Benj up and out of the syrup, the viscous brown dripping off him like engine oil, the floor a mess, sap splattering everyone except Perley, who saw it coming and stepped far back. One never drove a Cad with syrup on one's tan designer cords. One never, never saw the inside of Benj Carver's sugarhouse unless Benj Carver was dead in it.

While the squad wrapped a thick tarp around Benj, Amos wagged his finger at Perley. "You really hated him, didn't you?" he shouted. "Clipping three bucks like that out of you."

Amos's daughter Janice called Hugh two days later. "Can we talk?" she asked, her voice needful and sad. "It's about Dad and all these terrible things going on."

4

It is in the half fools and the half wise that the greatest danger lies.

—Goethe

SHE WAS WAITING for Hugh, and he was early. She opened the door with a smile on her lips, worry in her eyes. Janice Reed was an alluring mix of feminine confidence and female vulnerability, and Hugh was never late to see her. She was an editor of *Compute* magazine in Hampston, an hour's drive away, but she lived in Lyme, alone in a plain cabin with unplain electronics. That was one of her charms. The beauty with flowing, auburn hair, buttermilk skin and glancing green eyes manipulating bits and bytes. The woman with the long taming legs and blue pencils that corrected manuscripts from hotshot hackers.

He kissed her cheek, smelled the freshness of her skin, and felt her hand in his hold on tight after he tried to release it. He followed her the five feet to the open kitchen and watched her fix cinnamon herbal tea. They sat opposite each other at the shiny pine table next to the window, overlooking a cleared field lined with a thick stand of fast-growing hemlocks and plodding oaks. The oaks would win in the long run.

She leaned on the table toward him. Hugh leaned toward her. He thought of Eurydice and the magnetism she had that drew Orpheus to the heights of foolish impulse, the poor man. Listen to the gods. Don't look back. You'll trap her in hell. Eurydice had green eyes.

"Dad is worried sick," she said. "He doesn't let on, but he is."

"I know."

"He couldn't believe that he found Davy strangled like that. He didn't sleep that night. He had to tell the Chief about it, too, and then he thought the Chief was accusing him. You know Dad."

"I do, and I think he's great," Hugh said; Janice had a fleck in the green of her eye, and the flaw made her all the more absorbing.

"And then Benj. I couldn't believe it. It was terrible."

"I know Amos and Benj were at odds, and living so close like that."

"But they weren't really. Now Dad is accusing practically everybody for it."

"Janice, when something like this happens and it looks like it does, people can get sort of paranoid. You know what I mean? It's natural. That's what's happening to Amos. He wouldn't hurt a fly. But he's a great actor. And what a voice."

She laughed a little, smiled, rubber her fingers back and forth across the breadth of the table. "He's an old character. What can I say? He's my father."

"What can I do?"

She stopped rubbing her fingers and stretched out a hand to his, taking it. Asking something, but not knowing what, exactly.

She stood up and brought the pot and strainer back to the table. The loose tea type. "You know," she said, a perky elan replacing the worry, "Dad talked about Benj all night the day you found him. Everybody knows about that dispute over the land, but that happened centuries ago. Centuries. And they're still fighting about it. No wonder I took a twentieth-century job.

30

Hugh laughed. "I bet he loves that."

"He comes here, and every time he says, 'What are those things? Better mouse traps?' and I say, 'No, Dad, they're computers, word processors,' and then he says, 'Look like mouse traps to me.' It's a ritual we go through, like voting or something."

"The ritual species, whether we live in the twentieth century or not. The difference is that the twentieth century denies rituals and the others don't. But that doesn't change it."

"Hugh," she said, the tone changed again, "people don't know this too much, but thirty years ago or so Benj's sugarhouse burned down. He overheated the evaporator, and then he left to get more sap, and when he came back the whole thing was on fire. Dad and Benj were the same fighting cats back then, but Dad knew that Benj was nothing without a sugarhouse. So he gave him an old evaporator, and Benj built another sugarhouse around it. Does that sound like Dad would have anything to do with what happened to Benj?"

Hugh shook his head. "Of course not. I know that already."

"They were always at each other. I heard that Benj cut a birch down and it fell across Dad's land, right across the stone wall. Dad ranted and raved about how Benj was destroying his sugar lot, ruining the wall, this and that. Benj said that the birch was his and he could do anything he wanted with it and that Dad had to talk to God about which way it fell."

"Did he?"

"What do you think? Anyway, that night Dad went out before Benj could do anything and cut the part of the birch that was lying on his land into logs and hauled them away. He cut the tree so that what was left ended exactly right down the middle of the wall. Can you believe it?"

"What'd Benj do?"

"Well, *Dad* says that Benj then roped some young maples growing next to the wall on Dad's side and pulled them over the line. He tied them down and cut off the part that was on his own property. Crazy. He probably did it. Who knows?"

"They're going to miss each other."

Janice smiled. "Comrades in arms. I know they will. Old Benj. Who did it, Hugh?"

He drove back through town for a roll of stamps. The softness of her cool cheek lingered on, an aura around his lips. So did that female smell of hers. He never liked the myth of Eurydice and Orpheus, music and punishment, love and death. He'd rewrite it. Give the poor guy some reward for his hauteur, his frantic, passionate longing to see her emerge with him from the depths. The problem was that the gods were destroying him by destroying her, destroying him by subservience to dicta on high. The gods always did. Better to have the reward of snubbing the gods. Let *them* go to hell. Don't turn around or you'll never see Eurydice again. Rules, laws. Turn around! Look! Good gods should want that. Defiance. Expansion, not suppression. Inner strength, not outer authority. No, Hugh would rewrite it so that *because* Orpheus defied the rule of the gods not to turn around to see Eurydice his reward would *be* Eurydice. He swooned her with his music. All right, fair enough. But she was a honey. He ended up swooning himself. She was walking, breathing music. Feelable, so feelable. Better than notes. She had to have green eyes, too. Give her green eyes.

"Hi, Hugh. How are you, Hugh?"

Larry Sedgwick. He held his bundle of mail against his chest. It was full of every possible throwaway junk matter he could send for—catalogs for chocolates, fishing equipment, freighter trips to Europe, leather goods, Oregon strawberry jams, shoppers, pamphlets, coupons, free magazine trial subscriptions. He took it all home.

"Come on out here, Hugh, come on out here."

Hugh glanced at the postmaster and followed Larry out the door to privacy.

"Davy Tefler got strangled," he said.

"I know, Larry."

"He got strangled up there on Benj Carver's place. Somebody strangled him with plastic tubing, they use it for sap, collecting sap." He shook his head like a swatter. "It was horrible. I think it was horrible, don't you? I think it was horrible."

"I do, too, Larry."

Larry stepped closer. "Do you know what I think?" he asked, lowering to a whisper. "I think Benj Carver and Amos Reed planned it together. They planned it together."

"Well, Larry, I don't know," Hugh said, stepping back from the tall skinny man with the nimbus of frizzy hair.

"They planned it together. Then you know what happened? Benj got murdered." He shook his head again. "He got cooked in his own sugarhouse." His mouth stretched into a hyperventilated exposure of teeth. Not a smile. Nothing normal.

"I know, Larry. I was the one who found him."

"You did it?" he asked, his eyes whitening, leaning down, whispering, edging closer.

Hugh smiled. "No, Larry, I didn't do it. Otherwise, I wouldn't tell anybody, would I?"

He nodded. "Was he all cooked up?"

"No, but it was horrible, Larry."

"You know what I think? Amos Reed did it."

"Oh, I don't think so, Larry."

"Amos Reed did it because he didn't want Benj to tell they strangled Davy. That's why. So Amos killed two people, didn't he?"

"No, I don't think so, Larry, because Amos doesn't do things like that. You like Amos, don't you?"

"Amos gave me lessons in sugaring. I liked it. He took me up there and we sugared and he gave me some syrup I made. It was good. It was the best syrup I ever ate. Ever! I feel good but sometimes I don't and so I know people are strange. They look at me, but I look at them back!"

"I think you should."

Larry exposed his teeth again, stretching his mouth as far as he could. From a distance it was a smile, but up close a neutral reflex, eerie. Larry Sedgwick shuffled his Ichabod Crane legs back two paces and said, "I think somebody killed Benj because he was jealous. Aagggh! It was horrible! They drowned him first in the sap and it was boiling hot and it burned up his face and eyes and his tongue, his tongue got cooked, just like a cow's, didn't it? Then they lifted him up and pushed him all the way in the sap and boiled him all up, boiled him all up. Uuggaaah!"

With his detached, intense eyes he watched for a shocked reaction from Hugh, but Hugh said instead, "Well, Larry, it was horrible, just like you say. I have to get going now."

Larry took back his two lost steps and leaned closer. "Chief Atkins has a girl friend."

Hugh smiled.

Larry nodded again.

"You think so?"

Larry shook his head this time and exposed his teeth. "It's not his wife, either. He meets her underwater."

"Underwater?"

"They go out to the end of Chelsea Pond. I see them. They put on rubber suits. She's already there and he comes and puts on his rubber suit and then he goes into the water and dives down to her. They meet there underwater. They stay a long time and I stand there, they can't see me, and I watch them. Then he comes out first and then she comes out when he's gone. She comes out someplace else, but I can see her. He has to do that because he's the police chief. I don't think he should do that. I don't think he should do that."

"Why underwater, Larry?"

"Because he's the police chief. They have to meet underwater. You can come with me. I see them right there. They both wear those rubber suits, black rubber suits, black rubber suits. I see them. Do you want to watch them?"

"Well, maybe sometime, Larry."

"Do you want to eat lunch with me?"

"Some other time," Hugh said, easing away.

"They do it a lot."

"See you later, Larry."

Larry Sedgwick watched as Hugh gave him a half wave and walked to his car across the street. Then the angular, bean-pole man with a chestful of junk mail called out, "See you in the cemetery!"

"Speak."

"Quint."

"Get to it, Quint."

"How long can a man last in boiling maple sap?"

"Three to five seconds, give or take one or two. Instantaneous overload of nerves and arteries. Everything explodes—capillaries, veins, heart. Faster than a speeding bullet, if you're not a good shot. So that's how he was murdered."

"I thought you'd be curious."

"If you're not curious, you're already dead. Not a bad way, murder by maple syrup. Boils away all the fingerprints that lasers and infrareds can detect now, not to mention the victim."

"Not nice. Not much left intact but his buttons."

"You want to know about buttons."

"I don't want to know anything about buttons, Proctor. I want to know who killed the guy. You don't take baths in boiling sap."

"Nobody knows anything about buttons. I'll tell you about buttons. They're polyester. Plastic. They're all plastic after the Second World War. Before the Second World War they made them out of seashells, wood, bone, horn, nutshells. They did it for millennia. Now it's plastic.

"I don't want to know about buttons, Proctor."

"They make fifteen standard-size buttons for the clothing industry. You thought they made more. They make fifteen. Then they groove out some, nick some others, and it makes you think there are hundreds of varieties. Technology is clever, Quint, science is clever. Stick to it."

"I'm sticking to zippers and Zeno."

"You got buttons on your wallet pocket, buttons on your shirt front, buttons on your cuffs, on your skirt, on your dress, on your coat, your sweater, your hat, your robe, your purse, you got buttons all over the place."

"I don't wear dresses, Proctor, and I don't carry a purse."

"Eighty-one buttons are made every year for every button-mad American. Nobody knows about buttons. They sit around pushing their TV set all day. No wonder they don't know anything."

"You're crazy, too, Proctor."

"You're talking crypto-Lyme jargon again, Quint. Tell me about how they make syrup up there."

Hugh told what happened to Davy Tefler and Benj Carver. He pictured omniscient Proctor, the archetypal archivist, prowling back and forth in his paper-piled workroom, his telephone cord knocking one acid-free, gray storage box after another onto the floor, the contents scattered out of sequence, chaos returned. Did he ever *work* as an archivist? What did he do beside look up everything about buttons? Is that all he wanted to do, was know everything?

"Here's what you do, Quint. Get out of the woods and wait. Get a long-range telephoto lens and park yourself up there and wait. You got a crazy loose. He strangles the wrong guy first, and then he boils the next one. The question is simple: Did he kill the right one the second time or not? You won't know until you know what dollar bills are at stake. Find out who owns the sugar lot."

"Benj Carver's brother."

"Cain and Abel."

"His brother is waiting out cancer in Arizona."

"Then the lot goes up for sale."

"Proctor, the man just died."

"Eventually it goes up for sale. Think big, Quint. Einstein thinks big. Quint thinks small. Science, science."

"Science is guano, Proctor. Science is small, nothing but a collection of the rabbit pellets of life, a little fact here, a little fact there, measure this, weigh that. It's all parts, Proctor, science is spare parts. There's nothing whole."

"You want the holies, Quint, don't think murder."

5

I met Murder on the way.
        —Shelley

THE SHOT REVERBERATED in a muffled bounce in the bare trees as Hugh closed the door of his Audi. Instinctively, he crouched to his knees, ears cocked to follow-up noise. The shot came from behind the house: If you hear it, it missed.

He heard glass shatter, but at a distance. Maybe not. It wasn't his windshield.

He ran hunched down the path to Amos's sugarhouse. Twilight was edging out. No moon.

He rounded the corner of Amos's house; the sugarhouse was set back fifty yards. The chimney was steaming. Light bulbs filled the windows. One of them was shattered.

Hugh sprinted to a thick maple and waited. Nothing. "Amos?"

He dashed to a closer tree. His boots slipped an inch in the mud. He eased to the side. "Amos?"

Light shafted out the side window, shaped into an oblong chunk at a downward cast to the ground. He heard his breath. He ran to the corner of the sugarhouse, careful not to touch the wall, stepping flat-footed to keep the slush from sounding. At the window he ducked under the light shaft to the other side of it.

Then he moved in slow motion to the window, forced himself not to reach for the sill and expose his hand, forced himself to move like grass grows. Police training:

Never storm a door if you can find out what's inside the room first. Investigator: Patience, facts, go slow, no heroics. Remember the missing teenager; mother and father frantic; horror thoughts of religious cult kidnapping, brainwashing, torture; stalking down the motel room; three days watching with a telescope, sixteen-year-old daughter runs off with basketball star from another school; the girl is happy, for a week.

The inside of the sugarhouse enlarged in his eye—table with hot-plate burner, stack of logs, evaporator, broom, jugs.

Then he saw Rita, taut as glass, standing behind the door, waiting for it to smash open. Her fist clenched around a crowbar, her arms triggered to whack whoever rushed in at her.

Hugh backed away from the window and walked to the front of the sugarhouse. "Rita?"

"Hugh?"

"You all right?"

The crowbar clanked on the floor. She flung open the door. "Hugh, what's going on? Did you hear that? Am I glad you're here. Somebody took a pot shot at me!"

She stepped out, her face a twist of relief and fright. "Is Amos here?" he asked.

"No, he's bringing in the last load for today," she said, and followed Hugh back inside.

The glass was scattered on the thick, plank floor. The evaporator was still boiling, the fire roaring and crackling.

"Somebody shot out that window," she said, her face flushed with panic and from stoking the fire, the heat of the evaporator, the steam and radiation from the valves. "Could have *killed* me. I was standing right here in plain sight, just standing here watching the fire. Bam! Glass flying in. It scared the shit out of me, Hugh."

It was a rare admission. Rita was an iron bar herself. She hacked trees down for firewood like chopping up carrots. She pulled off her gloves and stuffed them into her hip pocket.

"You're all right? No glass hit you?"

She nodded. "What about that bullet?"

They stared at each other until Hugh said, "Did you see anybody?"

"Nobody. I ducked the hell behind the evaporator. I heard you call Amos, but it didn't sound like you. I wasn't taking any chances. You blame me?"

"Nope."

"So I grab that bar and stand behind the door."

"I know."

She stared at him; he had seen her through the window.

"I should've turned off the lights in here after that shot, but I was scared to move. Then I stood up in plain sight. Dumb. I don't know what I was thinking about."

"It's over and you did all right. You're not hurt."

"Who's doing this? OK, some people in town disagree, but they're going to *shoot* me, for God's sakes?"

"It's not you, Rita. It's Amos."

She craned her neck forward to understand.

"They thought you were Amos. Maybe."

"Why Amos?"

"Why Benj?"

"Maybe whoever it was saw that you weren't Amos, after all."

"Do I look like Amos in the first place?"

Hugh grinned.

They turned to the door as Amos bellowed through the trees: "Hey!" Then they smiled at each other.

Amos tromped through the soggy earth and dirty, leftover snow. He was swinging his arms in a march to San Juan Hill, trooper in the night, generalissimo.

"You hear that?" he shouted. "*Rifle* shot. Who did that? What's going on here?"

He strode through the doorway as Rita and Hugh parted the sea for him, old man Odysseus here to tell his tales. "I'm out there and I hear this shot. Who's shooting around here? I don't like it." He spotted the shattered window.

"That's what's going on," Rita said. Her mouth clamped tight.

"Who did this?" Amos demanded, staring at the shards on the floor. "Who's shooting up my place?"

"We don't know, Amos," Hugh said.

"What're you doing here?"

"I was coming out to see you and I heard the shot. It scared the shit out of Rita."

Amos stared at her, assessing the threat to her, the attack on his woman, his partner. He kept his fears bottled up, corked against the close call, but in the few seconds of staring silence he showed it in his eyes that he realized he was the target, not her, he was the one.

"I'm all right, Amos," she said, answering him.

He turned to Hugh. "Did you see anybody?"

"No, and it's too dark to look."

"We don't have to go far," Amos shouted, "Just go down to the PERLEY place over the hill and there you got him."

"We don't know that, Amos."

"I know it."

"What's he got to gain?"

"What do you expect? He comes up for weekends. WEEKENDS! I live here. That's the difference."

"Pretty big leap, Amos."

"He killed Benj," Amos shouted. "I saw him back away when he came clacking into ol' Benj's place there. Didn't want to get dirt on him."

"Well, I don't know anything about him," Hugh said.

"Well, find out!"

"I know something about him," Rita said, yanking on

her work gloves again, bending down to open the iron fire door under the evaporator, seeing if the blazing-red roar was getting too hot; it wasn't. "He lives on the Cape. Eastham, I think. Owns a construction company."

"They always cheat you," Amos said, taking the straw broom in hand and sweeping the glass into a neat pile, bending down with a dustpan to scrape up the shards. "That's why they're rich. You can't get rich without cheating somebody."

Rita glanced at Hugh. "Someone told me that Perley isn't liked much on the Cape. He's building down there faster than the Cape can stand. People are pouring in there. The water's bad and not enough of it, jamming housing in everywhere and turning it into a tourist carnival."

"Now I got to get a new window," Amos said. "Costs me money, you know."

"When they started those whale-sighting trips a while back, out of Provincetown and around, Perley fought it tooth and nail. The whole idea was to get people to see whales up close, show them that they're not something out of cardboard to shoot at. Maybe more people would put some pressure on Congress to stop that butchering. No, Perley fought that. They all fight it. I don't know. Maybe Amos is right. Maybe Perley is taking the offensive on this."

"I think I got an old window someplace in the basement."

"Last town meeting, he got up and talked against making a town conservancy on the far side of Chelsea. I talked for it. It didn't pass."

The fire raged behind Rita's blank face. Hugh knew about her. The years of fighting the likes of Perley. Losing twice as much as winning. Once she got the town to declare the back road to Hampton a scenic road, requiring that any changes to its rustic surface and overhanging maples, any bridges or culverts, had to go through exhaustive approval before the road crew could touch a leaf. It wasn't much of a road, it saved the town tax money. Some people on the road fought it, but the battle was a triumph for Rita. She made only a few enemies that time.

She grew more fiery over the years, and that was the rub. She used to win more in the old days. Now when she spoke for some conservation project, the automatic negative buzzer rang in the audience as soon as she stood up. They knew what she was going to say, and say hard. It grated. The more she lost the more she grated.

"I better call the Chief about this," Hugh said.

"What for?" Amos asked. "He won't pay for the window."

"Amos, this was a criminal assault. Either one of you could have gotten shot. Maybe both."

"What can he do? Turn on the siren?"

"It has to be reported."

"Why aren't *you* doing something about it? You didn't even find out how much syrup's selling down there."

"Twenty-nine fifty, if it's good."

"GOOD?"

Rita grinned, and Hugh stepped to the door. "Let me use your phone."

"Use my phone. The Chief is eating dinner, anyway. He eats dinner at breakfast. Tell him I said so."

"Right," Hugh said, walking toward the house.

Amos stood in the doorway and shouted, "Tell him to put his badge on right this time."

Hugh waved.

"I told you sugaring is exciting," Amos shouted.

The Chief drove up, slammed the door, and sauntered down the path past Amos's house to the sugarhouse out back. Rita told her story, then Hugh, then Amos. They spent twenty minutes discussing it, how it connected with Davy and Benj, what to do. Amos did the interrupting. The Chief rubbed his tongue on his side teeth and stared at Amos out the corner of his eye.

"So what are you going to *do* about it?" Amos shouted.

"We'll check it out."

"This ain't no supermarket, you know."

The Chief nodded and looked for something to look at in the sugarhouse. "You want to stay with your sister for a while?"

"What for?"

"Stay with Janice, then."

"What's the difference?"

The Chief managed his eyes up to Rita and Hugh.

"I got sap out there in the dark I got to bring in," Amos said. "Nothing stops sugaring. Tax money, that's what it pays for. Tax money. Not much. We through here or what?"

Hugh and the Chief walked to their cars out front, while Amos and Rita stayed behind to finish boiling off for the night. "They're a couple of nails," the Chief said. "You could pound them in a wall."

The Chief opened the door to the patrol car and leaned on it; he had something to say. "He tell you anything I should know?"

"Just what he told you," Hugh said, and pictured himself like the Chief some decades down the road. If he'd stayed in a Boston uniform, he'd be leaning on the open door and trying to shake off the abuse, too. He'd be taking orders to go into the Combat Zone for some hooker murder. He didn't like orders. He didn't like the time he arrested the crazy in an abandoned Roxbury warehouse who like to take the clothes off women with a razor blade. He never cut them. One woman let him do it twice.

What was he proving, being on the force? He couldn't even fill up the gas tank when his father told him. Do good by the rules. He tried, but orders were for coffee shops. Do something, his father said; this isn't a free ride because you're a Quint. A lot of sarcasm went into that; a lot of disguised arrogance, too. Go independent, he told himself. Do good, but go independent.

The Chief recommended and approved him for his license. Local police chiefs had to do that. State requirement. No approval, no license. He got jobs working for the district attorney. Investigating missing persons, lots of that. Investigating murder defendants on a public defender basis. Free-lancers saved the state money, and he didn't have to take too many orders.

The Chief said, "You got some time?"

"Some," Hugh said and nodded.

"The state is looking into this, but, hell, they won't do much. They're always doing too much else. I could use some help."

The man was tired. Handing out traffic tickets to tourists zooming through town took its toll long ago. "I'll check around," Hugh said.

The Chief shrugged. "Can't pay much. It's not Boston."

"Good thing."

The Chief sniffed approval and grinned, almost. It was a sign of relief, but nothing too official.

"What'd the autopsies show?"

"Nothing. Davy was strangled, but there was no sign of anything else. Benj was pretty much too messed up to show up anything. Now this," the Chief said, and jerked his head toward the sugarhouse.

6

You must lose a fly to catch a trout.
—Herbert

HUGH DROVE STRAIGHT to Janice's cabin and told her what had happened. She was dressed in a cobalt blue velour robe, her wet hair wrapped in a towel. Bare feet.

She stood staring at him as the description unfolded. He told her three times that Amos was all right, nothing to worry about. Rita, too. They were frightened, but they had sap to boil and that was what they were doing right now. He tried to get a smile out of her, but it didn't work.

Her questions were fast and concerned. They had the mark of the daughter protecting the father. She wanted to know why anybody would want to shoot at Amos. Hugh said that wasn't the case, not really. You had to look at it as a stark screen of events. A shot was fired into a window. Amos was not there. Rita was plainly in sight, but Rita may not have been the target. Maybe it was a prank, scaring old-timers doing their sugaring. Maybe it was totally meaningless; it didn't have any connection with anything because somebody just was out in the woods in a funk and fired at the lighted window without knowing or seeing anything.

Unconvincing. Janice edited paragraphs together on her magazine. She knew what connection was about. She knew about Davy and Benj.

She dediced to stay with Amos that night. She went into the bedroom to change, all the time asking Hugh about the shooting, what window it was, how far away her father was, who heard the shot, who saw anything.

She came out dressed in jeans and red-plaid shirt. She slipped on a crew-neck sweater. Her hair was brushed down, clipped back with two barrettes on both sides, still damp. She rushed back to the bedroom and then bathroom and this time came out ready to go with a small overnight case, all the time asking Hugh questions and listening on the run.

At the door she thanked him, reached up, and kissed him on his lips, her own lips wet, damp like her hair. It was startling and suggestive, self-shielding by the rush to get to her father. Hugh felt her after she was gone.

The next morning at six, Hugh parked his car out of earshot and walked down the gravel road to the Perley place. Mist hung heavy above the swamp on the left. The road had tightened in the cold night temperature. He made no noise.

He counted on the Perleys to be what Rita said—focused on hammers and screwdrivers and money. He counted on their being asleep. They wouldn't notice the blue jays and chipmunks squawking at Hugh from the limbs, tracing his progress from tree to tree, signaling intrusion, giving him hell.

He walked up the twisting driveway until he saw the Cadillac parked head-in. Then he raised his binoculars, wrote down the license plate number, and stuffed the paper in his jacket pocket.

The shout had a growling edge to it: "Hey!"

Hugh turned, erasing the sound, ignoring it.

"Hey, you!"

He turned back to the man jabbing his finger at him from the porch, filling the morning woods with threat. Hugh pointed his index finger at his own chest.

"Yeah, you," Perley said, and strode down the front

steps of his outsize cathedral-ceiling-and-glass house, painted Cape Cod gray.

Hugh watched the man police-walk toward him, his legs stepping long in the same designer cords he'd worn at Benj's sugarhouse. Perley kept his eyes on Hugh, kept his arms swinging fast. He walked past the white Cadillac, and from a distance he looked like a tall, manicured marionette. Up close he needed to command, his eyebrows thick and too horizontal, like the kind of mask a ventriloquist wears on TV shows. He hadn't shaved yet. His chin was a huge protrusion of bone.

"What're you doing here?"

"Birdwatching," Hugh said. "Sorry if I woke you up."

"You didn't wake me up. I saw you. You see that sign out there? Private."

"I must've been looking up. I thought I spotted a rose-breasted grosbeak."

"It says private. You were at Benj Carver's place, weren't you? When it happened?"

Hugh nodded.

"I own this place," Perley said. "When I come up here, I don't want people walking around. It's private."

"Sorry."

"You're walking on my driveway. You walk up other people's driveways? How do I know what you're doing? Maybe you're hunting."

Hugh backed off. Keep the future. Keep access. "No," he said, spreading his hands, surrendering, coming clean, smiling, "hunting season's later."

"Maybe I'm out hunting. On your own land you hunt anytime."

Hugh let it go.

"Maybe I'd take you for a deer or a red-breasted whatever-the-hell."

"Sorry."

Perley paused, staring hard, Attila the Hun weekending. "Yeah."

48

Hugh had seen the two types before. The summer people who came up and ingratiated their presence with benign deference, slumming a little flavor of the North Country, taking big city life off to talk with the natives about what should be done with the natives' country. Then the Perley type: The interlopers who cached their lives in the closeting woods. The ones who bought their escape with dollar bills instead of tickets to the church supper.

Perley said it again: "Yeah." He turned his head an inch, moved it up an inch, dark-eyed Doberman protecting the compound.

Hugh walked down the driveway, his binoculars bobbing against his chest. Only when he was halfway to the road did he hear Perley's steps fade back to the house. Perley watching. Perley pushing the trespassing sneak off his property with the power of his eyes alone. Perley the Terrible, triumphant again.

Hugh hadn't seen a rose-breasted grosbeak in years, and that was in Virginia. He couldn't feel the piece of paper in his jacket pocket, but he knew it was there.

Proctor Hammond hated the phone, but he always answered it.

"I need a trace."

"Don't call me. Call them."

"It's Massachusetts. Do you know the code name?"

"Of course I know the code name," Proctor said, and stopped.

"Well, are you going to tell me or what?"

"It's 'convention.' I suppose you want me to have them run it through, too. Do your legwork while you're up there in New Jungle counting ferns."

"Of course."

"Let's face it, Quint. You should've stuck to Cicero. You should've stuck with the One and the Many."

"Why, Proctor," Hugh said, angling the receiver away

from his ear as Proctor rammed his squeaky voice through it, "you surprise me. I never imagined you had any idea about Aristotelian analyses. I'm very impressed. But, of course, it wasn't Aristotle who conceived the problem. He just provided the best answer to why many things share one thing. Many trees all have treeness."

"Aristotle thought that fetuses started out looking like little babies in Mommie's uterus and just grew up into big babies until they were ready to pop out. He was all wet. We know better."

"He knew better about the One and the Many."

"Unimpressed. If he didn't know about little baby fetuses, he didn't know about big trees."

"If I thought that, I'd be a chessboard without the board, Proctor. You're confusing cumulative knowledge with noncumulative knowledge, wisdom with science. They go together like fire and ice. Classic mistake, Proctor. Classic. You can accumulate facts for science, and you can know more about something, scientifically, better today than yesterday, but just because Bertrand Russell came after Plato doesn't mean he's a better philosopher. Insights are timeless. Facts flit away with the sunset. Human nature stays the same."

"Try this, Quint. Light a match and stick your finger in it. Fact: Your finger will burn every time. Now tell me what you want from the Registry."

"The owner, what else?"

"Very good, Quint, very good."

"I want a run on this number," Hugh said, and gave him the plate number. "I think I know who owns it, but I want to make sure."

"Suppose he doesn't own it."

"I'll be curiouser. How do you get that code, anyway?"

"I call up a substation around here someplace like Waltham or Brockton and I say, 'This is Jim Anderson from the Registry of Motor Vehicles. Do you have the new code name?' Then the guy says, 'Yes, we have it.' Then I say, 'Will you please repeat it for me?' and he says, 'Convention.' I say, 'Thank you very much,' and hang up. Then I call up the Registry of Motor Vehicles and I say, 'Convention. Will you run a trace on this?' Simple."

Amos was hammering in the spare window when Hugh called out and then pushed open the sugarhouse door. He was slamming the hammer with all his might, thundering the noise through the shed. It was a wonder the glass didn't shatter again.

"Had it in the basement, just like I said."

"Janice gone already?"

"What do you want with her?" he shouted, smashing the nail one final time, punctuating his challenge with a blast, glaring at Hugh.

"I don't want anything with her. I just knew she slept over here last night."

"Gone to work. Some of us *work*, you know."

"I know, Amos."

"She told me you told her last night. Who told you to tell her?"

"I thought she should know. She's your daughter, Amos. I thought she might like to talk to you about it."

"Coulda waited 'til morning."

Hugh shrugged.

"Tell her to see me before I get shot, that it?"

"No, Amos, that's not it at all."

"What're you doing about it?" he shouted. "NOTH-ING."

"I'm talking to you about it."

"That's nothing."

"I came over to find that bullet."

"How do I know where it is? It missed."

"It missed Rita."

"I know it missed Rita. She's sleeping. Here till one o'clock last night, both of us *working*. If you got the sap, you boil it. You let it sit in the buckets more than a day and it'll start fermenting. I don't make syrup out of fermented sap. Some do, I don't."

"Did you get some sleep?"

"Sure, I slept. I got more sap to collect. Rita's coming soon. We WORK. Not like some people."

Hugh grinned and stepped to the wall opposite the shattered window. He leaned over the bench with the flannel filters and box of jugs and peered close at the wall. The slug had penetrated the blade of a cross-cut saw hanging on a nail and lodged in the pine stud behind it.

Amos watched.

Hugh put the saw on the floor, unclasped a pocket knife, and gouged out the slug. He held it up between thumb and forefinger.

"Why ain't the Chief doing that?" Amos asked, refusing to be impressed.

"Ask him."

"I'll ask him. Ruined my saw."

"You got another one in your basement?"

"Maybe."

"Maybe you should take a trip someplace, Amos. Do you good. Get away from here awhile. I don't want any of these hitting you instead of the wall."

"You threatening me?"

"No."

"I got sap still running. Comes only once a year, you know. Maybe six weeks. Big city people think that syrup's selling all year and so it comes all year. That's what *they* know. I lived here for CENTURIES and you tell me that I gotta take a trip. Benj slipped, that's what."

"He didn't slip."

"Place was a dump heap. He'd leave this window on

the floor. Dumb ol' boot. He wouldn't know how to sharpen a pencil. Couldn't figure out that ten hours of boiling burned up two cords sometimes. That's why he was always out of wood and there's sap waiting to boil."

"Davy didn't slip either, Amos."

"Never mind about Davy."

"You saw him. You're the one who spotted him."

"I got sap to collect."

The black Lincoln swerved into Perley's driveway as Hugh drove down the road from Amos's. He pulled even with the entrance, slammed to a stop, and read the license number out loud to himself. Then he headed down the road to Route 148. He stopped, wrote down the number, and stuffed the paper into his jacket pocket along with the slug. A Massachusetts plate.

Back home he took out the slug, placed it in an envelope, and sealed it. The piece of paper he put next to the telephone. He threw his jacket on the corduroy chair, sat down, and dialed Proctor Hammond.

"Have you got it yet?"

"I got it."

"The marvels of computers."

"No syllogism could do it."

"Who owns it?"

"Henry Perley of Eastham, Mass. On the Cape."

"I know."

"You want the address, I take it," Proctor said, and spelled it out. "And that's what you expected."

"Right. I got a better one."

"I'm not your two-bit dialing service, Quint. I'm not some finger in the yellow pages. I'm not your pet go-fer. I'm not your Gunga Din, Quint."

Hugh read him the number. "I'll call you."

"You always do."

7

For Knowledge, too, is itself a power.

—Bacon

SARAH BAYLORD HAD been the Lyme town clerk so long that she'd seen half the natives born there. She knew everything. So when Hugh came in for a tax map he wasn't surprised that she said in her birdy voice, "I see you're doing some work for the Chief."

He said yes, and a few other preliminaries necessary to get Sarah moving. Then he watched her little-old-lady-with-the-long-nose body straighten itself from the left-over teacher chair and walk to the gray map case. Hugh listened to the fountain of talk as she moved with the kind of all-knowing, self-conscious ploddiness that little old ladies on the inside track emitted. She knew that he knew that she knew everything, and she knew that he was watching her as a little old lady who knew what they both knew.

"The section on Chelsea is down here in the third drawer," she said as she bent down to examine the label, knowing damn well all the time that this was the right drawer. She pulled out the wide, narrow steel drawer on its creamy smooth rollers. "You have to put things back in the right places or nobody knows where they are when they need them, don't you know. The young kids these days, they don't do that. Heavens, nobody tells them to, nobody teaches them. I used to be a teacher. Well, you can't blame them, I guess, but they grow up and then nobody can find anything when they need to. It's here someplace."

Her blue and pink print dress was her wardrobe. Sarah Baylord never wore anything but print dresses and good tan leather shoes with soft soles. Gray hair cut short. Rosy baby-skin a thirty-year-old would envy.

She lifted up the starchy maps one by one. "It's here, don't worry," she said, and then keeping her head and eyes straight on the maps she added, "Terrible about Davy and Benj. I don't know what this town is coming to. 'Course, people forget back in forty-eight, right after the war, Johnny Jensen shot Bobby Wilson and killed him. Right after the war. Killed him. They were friends, too. They were supposed to be hunting and he shot him in the chest, right through the heart. They might as well shoot right through the heart of the town. It was out in the woods. They had an argument. This map is here, don't you worry. They had an argument over Betty Poole. She was a beauty. Pretty young thing. Now she's married to a pipe salesman in Ohio and has three kids. She left town after the shooting. I don't blame her. Everybody thought she flirted with them both. She didn't pull the trigger, but the people knew what she was doing. And right after the war, too."

She stopped at the sixth map and studied the identification. "Here it is," she said and shuffled it out, crinkling the stiff paper.

Hugh followed her through the doorway to the echoey, high-ceilinged, musty meeting room where she laid the map on top of the ten-foot, watermarked table. "The Pooles sold out and went to Florida. Then their blood thins out and they wonder what happens to them down there. Can't blame them. But they were better for the town than the next bunch buying in. People retire and then they don't pay their taxes and the town has to go through auctioning their land. Like the new bunch down by the Reed and Carver places. That's what you're looking at. I know that."

Finally, she looked up at Hugh with what should have been a knowing smile, but she didn't smile. She looked down again at the map and dotted her finger at the Perley acreage. "They drive around in a white Cadillac and they don't pay their taxes. And this isn't Taxachusetts, either. I know what they do. They keep the money in their money markets and get big interest on it until the town forces them to pay, I know."

Both the Reed and Carver places were listed at twenty acres each in blue facsimile ink, the Perley place ten acres. Hugh knew what the dual lines were, but he asked Sarah anyway.

"That's the railroad right of way," she said, dotting her hooked finger. "It goes right up between the Carvers and the Perleys. The old Boston and Maine Railroad. They still own it. I remember when the train came through town and we used to run down to the station and wave it in. Conductors were real nice then. They threw us candy every time they came through. People coming through. It was real nice. Now all you can do is walk along the old bed. They took out the rails, most of them. We used to hear the whistle coming, and we'd run down to the station. Julia Older wrote about it."

"What about this, Sarah?"

"That's an old logging road," she said, nodding, sounding the words in her chickadee voice. "Not much left of it. The Reeds used it in the old days. It goes up through the side of the Carvers and now the Perleys to 148. Perley came in here once. He's the new one down there. He wanted to look at this map. 'Is this official?' he asked me. He thinks I'm not official. Didn't care for him much, don't you know. Nothing's official to him if it's not in a big courthouse with a gold dome on it. We don't wear uniforms up here. I told him it was official if I told him it was official. I don't think he liked that much." She looked up again at Hugh. Her old watery eyes were powerfully gentle. This time she smiled. "He thinks he knows more than I do."

At home Hugh drew a rough sketch of Chelsea Pond and how the Reed, Carver, and Perley lands were stacked one, two, three behind it. He drew the Boston and Maine right of way and the old logging road that cut through the properties, the railroad moving on west, the logging road heading north to Route 148. With Xs he marked where he and Amos found Davy Tefler and then Benj's sugarhouse. He drew a small box for Amos's sugarhouse.

On either side of Amos's land, the shoreline was rocky and edged Chelsea with steep cliffs. It was a natural division of the land, giving the Reeds the only access to the water for at least a quarter of a mile on either side. No wonder the feud lasted as it did. The pond on this side curved in a lazy slide of a half-moon. The rest of the lake formed a gigantic W. At two points the surface stretched for great absorbing expanses of blue, peaceful, lapping water that healed. At the same time, the pond had intimate rocky coves and seclusions. This was a treasure of a lake. The woods grew to the edge of the water and kept the few cabins and cottages scattered around the lake out of sight. Amos's own place was set back enough from the shore to forbid the crassness of shore-hugging tourism that ruined places like this.

Hugh studied the sketch. He thought of Actaeon and Artemis. The hunter owned fifty loyal hunting dogs, whimpering and friendly companions at home but savage beasts on the stalk. He was out one day in the thick woods hunting for a stag, letting his dogs catch a scent, watching them scurry through the hemlocks with their noses sniffing high and low. It was a great day for a hunt, but he and the dogs were having no luck.

The hunter leaned against a tree, and there in the short distance he saw a woman bathing naked in a crystalline stream. Mesmerized, entranced, he stared at her. Artemis, twin sister of Apollo, was bewitchingly beautiful. The water coated her with glistening appeal. Her skin sparkled in the streaking forest sunlight glowing like a spotlight on her beauty. She washed herself like the virgin she was, her nakedness as private as only innocence allowed.

Actaeon knew that he must not violate this privacy, but the highlighted beauty in the shrouded woodlands held his attention beyond all attempt to avert his gaze. And now the hold turned to a savoring, and Actaeon watched with ever-deepening consciousness, waiting for the beauty to finish washing her hair, to flip it upward and back, to turn his way so that he may see what she forbade all others to see. He watched her cup her hands in the rippled stream and pour the water once more onto her shiny arms and legs. He watched her kneel on an angled ledge to drape her hair into a pool and weave her strands melodically through the clear water. He stared at her soft lines in the quiet distance, the femaleness of her appeal.

All the while he stood hidden in the backdrop shadows and the unspeaking trees. Then she flipped up her hair, and its strands sprayed diamond lights that haloed her presence. She stood up and turned his way, and Actaeon stole the virgin's beauty entirely.

When Artemis saw the hunter in the thieving dark shadows, she allowed only the moment of searing revelation of this theft to take root. Then, as protector of all virgins, avenger of trespass and desecration, Artemis changed Actaeon into a stag. She remained at the edge of the sumptuous water for Actaeon to see her beguiling beauty and waited for the hunter's loyal dogs to catch the scent. Actaeon could do nothing, neither rush forward to sweep his arms around the woman and carry her away nor command his dogs to stay their search. He wished to escape to the high woods, but as a luring man hidden by the form of the vulnerable stag he was held fast to the terrifying beauty. This goddess who must not be violated watched as the quickened dogs caught the scent and bounded through the woods in yapping, passionate chase. They tore the stag to pieces.

Hugh thought the lightfooted scurrying was a dog. Dogs followed their noses through his place now and then, running loose in the woods and fields, seeing and smelling what they could see and smell. He didn't think much about it until the sound stopped too long for a dog to lift its leg. Dogs on the loose never stood still long.

He got up and looked out the window. Nothing.

The Russells' setter was always running through, sniffing Hugh's back porch, galloping through the front brush, stopping, sniffing, stopping, sniffing. His paws on the gravel around the foundation clicked and clacked on scheduled route. The setter was a frisky sight, but it wasn't trained. The Russells never used it for hunting, never could. The dog always left his mark on three strategic oaks around Hugh's place, and that was all.

It didn't sound like the Russell dog.

When the shot blasted through the window, Hugh was back in his chair. The shot exploded through the room with a thunder. Invisible, violent, thunder from an invisible lightning. The glass collapsed and sprayed the floor.

Hugh's insides panicked into a vacuum.

He lunged to the floor.

And rolled to the wall.

He waited for the house to crush him. He curled into

womb-protection, buglike, a primeval beetle ahead of its future, hiding his defenseless gut. Expendable arms wrapped his head. Wrapped the nerve center.

The house stood. The glass finished shattering.

He waited for the pain.

It didn't come; he ran like a crab along the wall. Below the windows. He got to the kitchen and pressed his back against the wall.

He heard his breath.

He waited for the second shot.

When it didn't come, he shimmied up the wall, and at the right level he turned his head and edged his line of sight out the window.

Nothing.

No movement. No sound.

He remembered crouching in the tunnel of alley darkness in Saturday-night Dorchester and how the shot reverberated like an oscilloscope against the brick canyon. His partner was blocking the other end of the L-shaped alley. He shimmied up the sooty wall to see over the iron trash-dump, and all he saw was an endless tube of black. He heard his breath and he felt his heart and he smelled the moldy, stinking bin of trash and garbage that the rain and rats and marauding dogs let rot. He waited for footsteps and they didn't come at him and they didn't head out. He listened for the telltale panic, reached for it, knew it was there in the midnight, the fast cancer eating the guts out of the punk. Nothing. Where the hell did he go? Waiting it out forever. His partner had him, but he didn't. Don't move. Make a move and you're dead, because the scrim of light is behind you and what moves is you, not the light. What moves gets shot. How the hell did he get away? He knew the territory. Slipped through a rathole and he's home free. Nothing to track. Black on black. Too many corners and options, and in his territory he knows all the options. He's got the lead.

Now Hugh ran on all fours to the back door and eased out, eased the door back in place, eased down the steps. Around the corner.

He studied the bank of woods opposite the window.

He wanted to *smell* the tracks.

The woods were an abrupt wall that defeated the eye at the first flank of tree trunks. It was too thick and dark.

He waited, and still nothing. He could be seen. Maybe in the alley he was seen, but whoever had the gun knew better. Smart.

Hugh stepped out: The head knows what the body doesn't. It was over, but his gut was tight against another roaring smash of glass and ear, another rip into the calm of his body.

He walked to the edge of the woods. This would be the spot. A clear shot. He saw himself at the edge of the window. It was a bad shot at him, a good shot at the window.

Which one?

It could come anywhere back from here. Just a straight sight needed.

He listened intently, an aggression on the silence. Standing still. Moving his head in inches. Nothing.

Patience.

Scraping birches. Breezes through the needles. It was all in the air.

He walked back to the cabin. Halfway there he stopped without turning around and listened.

He went inside, closed the door, locked it. The shattered window was pouring night air inside. He had some pine boards out back. He'd have to hammer them across the window, maybe stuff the gaps with old fiberglass insulation, tape it, hang and tape a plastic sheet.

He'd have to sweep up the shards. Wicked, angular sheets of glass stuck in the frame; take them out.

That had to wait. He wanted to find the slug. The room

was bigger than Amos's sugarhouse, and he had to search longer for the splintered impact. He stood at the window and estimated the patch of wall where it had hit.

He found it next to a knothole, almost missing the spot because impact, too, looked like a knothole. He gouged the slug from the wood with his pocketknife.

Hugh's stomach tightened, and he felt the after-shakes making their presence, the nausea that came with confronting the missed possibilities he held in his hand. Then the anger. Defiance. Retribution. The need for compensation for this outrageous assault on his person and his privacy. He was no longer a public uniform, no longer beholden to institutional objectivity. It was the anger that calmed him.

The slug looked like the same gauge as the one he'd dug out of Amos's sugarhouse. It was twilight, too.

8

THE WOODS HAD deadened the sound of the shot; the chances of anyone hearing it were slim. The chances of anyone reporting it to the Chief were slimmer. Shots were fired now and then; country life was like that. The same sound in Boston would ignite a thrash of angry, protective, fearing, belligerent calls to police and neighbors, and sirens would be blaring up and down the streets. Not in Lyme.

If Hugh told the Chief about the shot, Sarah Baylord would find out. Sarah Baylord found out everything. Sarah Baylord believed in the Freedom of Information Act in reverse; the whole town would know and wouldn't have to ask.

Hugh decided not to tell anyone.

In the morning Proctor Hammond told Hugh that the Registry of Motor Vehicles listed the owner of the Lincoln as Thomas Fratacelli, gave Hugh the address, and said, "You have to boil ninety-seven percent water out of the sap."

"What has that to do with Fratacelli?"

"Nothing. You don't need anything more about Fratacelli. I'm telling you about sap. You wanted to know the name behind the license plate on the Lincoln you saw and that's it."

"Occam's Razor."

"You can call it anything you like, Quint. The fact remains the same. Thomas Fratacelli is the registered owner of the Lincoln."

"William Occam congratulates you on your reserve. A medieval type, he was. Don't do with more when you can do with less. Take your razor and slice off the excess. Get to the heart of the matter."

"Exactly. Good-bye."

"Wait."

Proctor sighed immeasurable tolerance into the phone.

"You boil off ninety-seven percent of the water?"

"That's what I said. You want me to repeat it and, therefore, you want me to violate my friendship with William of Occam. You ask too much. Occam's Razor, Quint, Occam's Razor."

"*Touché,* and I see how your mind works."

"Nobody sees how my mind works."

"I ask how much maple syrup sells for down there, and now you end up telling me how much water you have to boil off."

"Good syrup weighs eleven pounds a gallon. Good syrup consists of thirty-five percent water, sixty-two percent sucrose, one percent invert sugar, one percent malic acid."

"I got shot at last night."

Silence.

"True."

"Quint," Proctor said (could it be concern, genuine worry, actual solicitude?), "watch yourself. You got a loony up there. A killer. You're a snag. Killers don't like snags. It was a warning shot."

"Maybe."

"It was. You're a periphery. You get deeper and you're going to be central. Killers aim for bull's eyes."

"Thanks, Proctor."

"You don't know who's behind it."

"I'm working on it."

"You think this Fratacelli has something to do with it, but you're not sure."

"Who knows? I've got to check him out. He's an outside element hooked up with an inside connection. Henry Perley. What's that do for you?"

"Nothing."

"Fratacelli?"

"He drives a Lincoln. Check that. He owns a Lincoln."

"Yeah, right. I need some answer on this."

"Socrates was killed because of questions."

"That's philosophy, Proctor."

"That's fact, Quint."

That night Hugh drove up Route 148 to take a look at the Perley place again at a distance. And the Lincoln. At the cutoff to the gravel road, the Lincoln swerved onto 148 and sped past Hugh.

"Judas."

Hugh turned onto the gravel road, jammed off his lights, whipped the Audi into a pebble-kicking, paint-nicking turn-around, and peeled back onto 148, lights still off.

The Lincoln was out of sight.

Hugh turned on the headlights and pressed forward over the rolling asphalt. At the third roll he saw the Lincoln ahead, the characteristic taillights in three-section grouping. Fratacelli was heading toward Hamilton. He could turn there toward either Claytonville or Lewiston. Chances were nil, but who knows? What was in Claytonville or Lewiston? Nothing.

Fratacelli headed straight through the blinking yellow light in Hamilton village.

Hugh slowed, kept back. He was only a couple of

headlights in the Lincoln rear view mirror. Just before the Hamilton intersection he switched on the left turn signal, turned the wheel halfway, shut off the headlights and turn signal. Then he whipped the car back straight ahead and let the Lincoln disappear over another rise.

He held back and turned on the headlights again. At the top of the second rise he saw the Lincoln taillights on a downward straightaway. He kept back. Fratacelli was heading toward Route 101 probably, another fifteen minutes of back roads. The trees hadn't leafed out; they were bony stuff along the two-lane road, curving and winding.

Everybody was followed on country roads. Once you got on you stayed on. You didn't think someone's following you unless you were used to it.

Fratacelli wasn't used to country roads. He took turns too slow, too much braking.

They passed through Greenton, nothing but a store and gas station, serve yourself. Hugh pulled to the curb and watched the Lincoln drive on. He turned off the ignition: no headlights, no parking lights. He waited for the Lincoln to disappear; it wasn't going anywhere but straight. Where else was there?

He turned the key and caught up to the Lincoln a mile later. To Fratacelli eyeing the mirror, Hugh was just another local yokel stopping to buy beer, then a different local driving some damn place.

When the Lincoln red-lighted at the stop sign before turning onto 101, Hugh let another car slip in between. Then he followed Fratacelli the ten miles to Route 3. Once on 3 the Lincoln held steady at fifty-five miles an hour until it crossed the state line. The highway was a funnel out of the New Hampshire wilds to Route 128 that rimmed Boston with scores of multilayered, high-tech companies.

"Boston," Hugh heard himself say. He's headed to Boston.

For twenty minutes he followed the Lincoln as it sped up to seventy once in Massachusetts. You drove any way you wanted in Massachusetts. Past the granite quarry, over the Concord River, past the Burlington Mall.

Fratacelli turned onto Interstate 95. Hugh followed, curving around the cloverleaf, watching the tallights two cars ahead.

"Judas!"

On the straightaway the Lincoln shot ahead like a rocket. Hugh floored his Audi—eighty, eighty-five, ninety.

The Lincoln bolted ahead into the left-hand lane, a streak of black-encased red.

One hundred miles per hour.

Hugh glanced at the speedometer. He squeezed the wheel. "Judas," he said, and then sliently: "Goddamn bastard."

Does he know?

Suddenly, the Lincoln braked, the taillights blasting red.

Hugh braked, holding back a quarter mile. The difference was that Fratacelli couldn't see the Audi taillights.

The Lincoln slowed to fifty-five, then fifty, forty-five, forty. Still in the left-hand lane. Forcing cars that seeped between the Lincoln and the Audi to pass on the right.

Including Hugh.

Hugh swerved two lanes to the right and passed Fratacelli at fifty-five. He turned to the far right lane and kept a steady pace, catching the lagging big Lincoln finally in his rearview mirror.

He edged to the shoulder and let the car drag to a stop. No braking, no taillights so Fratacelli wouldn't notice with the rest of the traffic rushing down the lanes. The guy was either trying to shake Hugh or he was paranoid, his usual routine. If paranoid, he had a reason. If he had a reason, he was worth following.

The Audi crept to a stop.

The Lincoln shot ahead again. Left lane. Then the right lane to pass some bewildered bastard. Left lane again.

Hugh spun the Audi off the shoulder and wove in and out of the traffic.

Sixty-five, seventy-five, eighty-five, ninety-five.

Let no son-of-a-bitch get in the way.

One hundred for two miles heading past the I-93 junction toward the seacoast.

Then the Lincoln blasted its taillights again and swerved to the right, hacking off the traffic, forcing on a battery of taillights as the big car headed in a dive-bombing angle to the I-93 turnoff.

Hugh cut to the right, slowed, watched the Lincoln tilt around the crescent turnoff and disappear onto I-93. It didn't matter. He knew the taillight pattern. He'd catch him.

The Lincoln was a fading streak in the distance. One hundred again.

Hugh floored the Audi. When Fratacelli braked for the Storrow Drive turnoff, Hugh had him. He grinned and said, "Shit." Easy.

The traffic held the Lincoln down. Hugh let three cars, then four, intervene. He pulled another fake turn and kept the Lincoln in sight.

Fratacelli headed onto Route 2, through Cambridge, around the new rotary, and through the red light, up and over the hill with the night lights on the Grace and Raytheon Corporation signs. When the divided highway meshed into two lanes before squeezing into the Concord woods, Fratacelli braked and whipped the wheel around.

The Lincoln jerked into a sharp U-turn and headed back toward Cambridge, fast.

Hugh reached the end of the divider, saw an opening, and snapped off the headlights. He whipped the Audi into a U and floored it, lights back on.

The Lincoln streaked back the four minutes to the rotary. Hugh lagged behind and watched Fratacelli circle around the rotary to the west side of Route 2 again, only he kept going. Around again he went, twice.

Clever, paranoid son-of-a-bitch. He got Hugh sucked into the rotary too soon. But did Fratacelli know it?

Hugh turned off to Milton. The Lincoln completed the second circle and headed onto Route 2 west again. Fast.

Hugh whipped the wheels across the double line and floored it to the rotary, turned onto Route 2. The Lincoln lights were shrinking fast in the left lane. He caught up, just enough.

By the time Fratacelli reached the other end of the divided highway, Hugh had let a scattering of cars intervene again and kept his Audi on the right side, just another pair of anonymous headlights to the Lincoln rear view mirror. He followed the big car into the woods, turned left when it did, wound around the dark country lanes where Paul Revere and the Minutemen had scrabbled in revolutionary panic, steered over the asphalted terrain that Thoreau and Emerson and all the other Concord Olympians walked.

Hugh faked another turn and then finally caught up to the Lincoln again.

Suddenly, Fratacelli right-angled into a barely-visible driveway. Home.

Hugh drove on by.

Around the next bend he pulled into another driveway, reversed, and eased back down the road. He turned out the headlights and coasted into a side clearing: no braking, no taillights. Fratacelli's mailbox stuck out next to the driveway. Probably no name on it. Too dark to see that far.

The man would come out the driveway and chances were he'd turn east to Boston. Hugh'd stay put on the west side of the driveway, back enough to be nobody, close enough to see.

He slid down in the seat. The extra-tinted windows helped; they were better in the daytime. Headlights poured in too much. The traffic wasn't much here. He'd wait.

The man had training with cars. Down the wild goose chase at a hundred. Slowing to forty in the left lane. Secret Service stuff. Twice around the rotary. Hell, it wasn't anything new. Paranoid. Taking precautions. Something to hide. Too many movies.

"Judas."

The Lincoln must have turned around in the driveway someplace. It came squealing out and onto the road, headed east, and disappeared around an outcropping of trees and boulders. Getting away.

Hugh peeled onto the asphalt and caught sight of the Lincoln on the third bend. It wasn't the man's house. Smart.

Fratacelli turned not onto Route 2 but onto another country road running a stop sign at the junction.

Hugh watched the Lincoln turn. Then he jerked to a quick stop and drove straight on through. Out of sight he jerked into a driveway, reversed, and burned rubber. He caught the telltale lights as the big car moved into the village center with the mercury-vapor lights. He watched the man pull the Lincoln to the curb, get out, and enter the general store. Hugh pulled his Audi behind a truck on the diagonal and watched out his side-view mirror.

Fratacelli walked out with a small bag in his hand. He walked as if he were moving faster than he was, hands and arms swinging farther than necessary. Maybe six feet tall. Maybe gray hair; hard to tell in the night light; maybe blond, probably gray. Bony-legged. Jerky stride. Cocky.

He yanked open the car door and threw in the bag.

That was all Hugh could see.

The Lincoln squealed its tires around in a U and headed fast past Hugh, slumped out of sight.

Then Hugh waited until it was gone before turning the key. Ignition meant parking lights on. He was going to have to fix that sometime. He floored it and caught sight of the Lincoln as it wound back into the crowded woods with the upper class castles set deep in the scurvy woods, set away from casual view.

He followed the Lincoln back to the same driveway. So it *was* Fratacelli's place. He parked the Audi in the same turnoff. And waited.

He remembered that surveillance, a plant, on a drug case in Dorcester, and it was December and *cold*. Out of uniform. Huddling in a parka and a goddamn blanket in the goddamn car he couldn't turn on for heat. Turn it on and out goes the exhaust. Exhaust makes smoke signals. No smoke signals allowed. He watched the smudgy front door, the alley, the side windows, the hookers, the bums. All night he watched, getting sleepy, forcing the concentration. You lose concentration and you lose the prey. Doze off and they slip out. They don't pick the time. It just works that way. But they didn't slip out. In December? He waited all night. He saw the scum. All he did was watch. All night it was cold, and the prey was inside, warm.

9

Saint abroad, and a devil at home
—Bunyan

IN THE MORNING Hugh felt like the Russian army had marched through his mouth. No wonder Napoleon lost the eastern front. The quartz clock read 6:47. Too many trees for the sun to break through at the sunrise angle.

His bones ached. So did his stomach. He needed coffee. And a croissant. A nice, fat, buttery croissant, the kind that's crisp and sturdy, not these mealy-mouth, flaky-pastry fakes. Croissants were rolls, for Christ's sake, not puff pastry. You're supposed to use your teeth with croissants, they're not canned peas. And they have to be made with butter, great slabs of sweet yellow butter folded in. Buy them at a bakery, too, and not just the oven shops where they get them frozen, made in a monstrous factory, and then shoved into the oven to heat up. Get them at a real bakery and then you *smell* them baking, all that nutty bread-baking aroma of trays and trays of croissants. Eat them fresh, but not heated. Nobody French heats croissants. You want soggy croissants, go ahead, heat them. Then you sit there and alternate drinking some fresh-roasted *café au lait*, eating some croissants, then some coffee. Taking your time. Goddamn, he was hungry.

Three cars passed in the next half hour. Maybe Hugh'd be waiting until noon. Maybe longer. Who knows? He could *die* of hunger. And for what? Fratacelli drives his

Lincoln out of Perley's place. The man drives like a Fury to lose whoever is following him, but he doesn't even know who's following him, if *anyone's* following him. It all proves he lives here. So what? Hugh knew that from Proctor.

Some tangle was trying to choke out Amos, but what? It made sense about Perley; if you're used to money schemes somewhere, you look for money schemes everywhere, even right where you live. So how did he tie in with Fratacelli? But is Perley going to tromp out in the night woods and fire through Hugh's window? Sure, why not? Or hire somebody. Keep that in mind—or hire somebody. Trying to scare Hugh off. But anybody could do that. Look at Amos, the way he cut the part of Benj's birch that fell over his property, and chopped it up for spite. You couldn't put anything past him. Sometimes the obvious was right *because* it was obvious, and if Amos was anything he was obvious. Rita, too, smoldering at the likes of Perley and his herd moving into the territory. But someone shot at her in Amos's sugarhouse, with Amos gone collecting. Naw, not Amos. He wasn't that crazy. It might as well be Sarah Baylord or Larry. Judas, he was hungry.

The Lincoln squealed out the driveway onto the road. Hugh reached for the ignition key and let out, "Ha!" He held back, waited for Fratacelli to disappear around a curve, and then he turned the key.

He followed the Lincoln out of the trees and onto Route 2 where it widened into eight divided lanes, thickening with morning traffic. Good. The thicker the better. At night he was a set of nameless headlights. In daylight he was the whole car.

He stayed behind on the diagonal. When Fratacelli got blocked in, Hugh passed him on the far right lane, then dropped back again. When Fratacelli squeezed through a yellow-red light at the Alewife T station, Hugh stopped.

Nothing to worry about; Fratacelli wasn't going anywhere beyond the jam up at the next rotary. Boston was good for something.

He followed the Lincoln across the Charles River and onto Storrow Drive. Three minutes later he turned off, circled around Boston Common, and watched Fratacelli turn onto Joy Street at the edge of Beacon Hill and double-park.

Who didn't double-park in Boston? Hugh did the same and blinked on his emergency lights. He watched Fratacelli get out and walk his cockatoo walk across the street. He was carrying a brown manila envelope. He climbed the stairs to an old brick townhouse and entered the building. Hugh watched and smiled. It was a drop-off. It was worth no croissants.

Less than a minute later Fratacelli ran down the steps, got in the Lincoln, and squealed off.

Hugh rehearsed what he was going to say to the secretary/receptionist/long-haired, curvy Cerberus. These town houses were now offices and some of them, in keeping with the blinder tradition of blue-nose Beacon Hill, kept their names unengraved upon their front doors. So he would run frantic up the stairs, swing open the doors, and say breathlessly, "I thought I just saw Thomas Fratacelli come in here. At least I thought that was his car." And she would say, "Yes, you just missed him." Or she'd say, "No, that wasn't Thomas Fratacelli, that was Joe Odysseus." Then he'd say, "I was supposed to drop off an envelope for him, but I left it in his office." Then she'd say, "Oh, that's all right, he just dropped it off." She wouldn't question until later why he was there in the first place. Then he'd say, "It's supposed to be for . . . for . . ." and here he'd churn his hands in a desperate effort to conjure the right name. Then she'd say, "Mr. . . ."

He got out of the car, ran up the steps and stopped. He

had what he wanted without the stage production. The letters on the glass door read Perley and Unger.

After Hugh devoured two Newbury Street croissants and *café au lait*, he headed back to Lyme, stopped at his place to shave and clean up, and drove to Amos's.

Amos and Rita were still sugaring, the sugarhouse still steaming, the aroma still sweet and marly. Amos was smoothing a felt filter. Rita was carrying in logs. The evaporator was bubbling like a baby. The fire underneath was roaring in a hush.

Amos got right to it. "You know anything you didn't know yesterday?" he said, looking up as Hugh came in and latched the wood-slat door shut.

"Hi, Rita."

She nodded, smiled, and rolled her eyes toward Amos.

"*Well?*"

"As a matter of fact."

"Guess that takes care of the month, don't it?"

"I see you got a window back in."

"Sure I do. Can't let the wind come blowing through here, ruin my syrup."

"Amos," Rita said, "no measly wind is going to ruin your syrup. Hugh isn't that dumb."

"Thanks, Rita."

"Anytime," she said, opened the firebox door with her gloved hand, and tossed in two logs like kindling.

"Well?"

Hugh leaned against the wall. "Have you seen a black Lincoln in Perley's place lately?"

"I seen it. It's been coming here," Amos shouted, fitting the filter in the top of a funnel can. "You know, some of these guys never even filter the stuff. They just pour it right in the jug. Some of them, they filter it once. Once! I filter it TWICE. That's why I make good syrup. Then people wonder what that black molasses stuff is on the bottom of their jug, what's that stuff floating around. So I filter it *twice* and nobody sees anything. *That's* good syrup. This isn't that corn syrup junk they make with half water, half chemicals, you know."

"I know that, Amos."

"What about it?"

"I found out who it is. Thomas Fratacelli. You know him?"

"What?" Rita said, head jutting forward, eyes staring. "Out of Boston?"

Hugh nodded.

"Who's Fratacelli?" Amos shouted.

"That slippery son-of-a-bitch," Rita said.

"I never hear nuns cuss like that," Amos said. "Yeah, I seen that Lincoln up there at Perley's."

"If he's the one I'm thinking of," Rita said, "he'd bulldoze the White Mountains into a parking lot. He'd put a hotel on Georges Bank. He'd put condominiums on Hatter's Island. Now he's trying to get his claws into the Isles of Shoals. Make it a Coney Island. Sure, I know Fratacelli. He doesn't give a damn about gutting the best land we got because he doesn't live there."

"What's he doing up here?" Amos asked.

Rita's eyes and mouth tightened. "Two to one he's hooking up with Perley. Yeah, I'm beginning to zero in on Perley, all right. It's looking bad on him. Fratacelli and Perley go together, and so does money and murder. Fratacelli's trying to get Perley to develop something, get his claws in up here. He'll rip it up before anybody knows what hit him. I've seen it happen. He gets in the closet with somebody, somebody local like this Perley character, and then he backs them with big money. You know about it."

"I don't know about this Fratacelli," Amos said.

"He's a sleazy son-of-a-bitch."

"Well, get him out of here!" Amos shouted.

"It's a free country, Amos," Hugh said. "People can travel where they want."

"Not on my—"

"He's behind all this, isn't he?" Rita said to Hugh, cutting Amos off.

"Behind *what?*" Amos shouted.

"You know what—Davy and Benj. Shooting through this window here. *Your* window. Who knows what mob he's hooked up with?"

"What mob?" Amos shouted.

"That's what I just said."

"I know what you just said."

"I don't want to talk about it anymore," Rita said. She stalked through the back door and shuffled around for more logs to carry in, making noise, throwing things.

" 'Course, she doesn't want to talk about it," Amos shouted. "You see how she *talks* about it."

Hugh shrugged.

"Women get so danged riled up."

"She got shot at, Amos."

"We all get shot at. I got shot at in a WAR. How can I finish the season with all this going on? I got to make my tax money, you know. I don't do this for fun, you know that, don't you? I gotta WORK for a living. I just don't sit around all day dreaming all that sap is going to turn itself into syrup. What do you think?"

"Is it still coming?"

"It's still coming. It's a good season. Slow today. Too cold. But it'll come lots tomorrow. You can't just let it set in the tank. You got to *boil* it. You want good syrup, you got to *boil* it right away. She don't give it to you when you're good and ready. She gives it to you when SHE's good and ready."

Hugh nodded, tapering the conversation with a silence.

"I got shot at in a WAR," Amos shouted. "Bullets

don't scare me now. They scare me when they hit me, and then it's too late to be scared."

Rita came back carrying two chunks of wood. She dropped them on the floor, opened the firebox door, and shut it. As conciliation, she asked Amos, "Is it getting too hot?"

"Yeah."

So she reopened the door and threw in another two logs to quiet the fire. "The Chief find out anything?" she asked Hugh.

"The CHIEF?" Amos shouted. "The Chief's got retirement heaven on his mind. What's he going to find out here on earth?"

Rita glanced at Hugh and shook her head.

"Give him some time," Hugh said.

"Give him a year to tie his shoe."

"He's trying to get the State Troopers on it."

"To tie his shoe?"

"Amos!" Rita said.

"Last I heard, the Chief was changing to shoes with no laces."

"Amos, he's just as concerned as you are," Hugh said.

"How do you know?"

"He asked me to help some."

"*I* asked you to help."

"I know that, Amos."

"WELL?"

"It's all the same problem, Amos."

"It's not the same people."

"Amos," Rita said, "go get some more sap."

"You calling me a sap?"

"Amos!"

"She is, ain't she? She's calling me a *sap*."

"No, she's not."

"She's changing the subject."

"Yes, Amos, she's changing the subject."

"Thought so." Then he smiled.

Amos dipped a thermometer into the bubbling syrup in the broad-faced evaporator—215 degrees. Not hot enough. He boiled to 221 because 221 made better syrup than 220. Amos Reed never took off syrup at 216 or 217 degrees. Some others did, especially in short years. They ended up making thin syrup; they ended up getting more volume, but it was syrup that disappeared right through the pancakes. Too thin. It took Amos Reed another half hour to get the temperature up another 5 or 6 points, but that's the way he sugared. Thick syrup. It stayed on the pancakes. It wasn't short-boiled and thin, and it wasn't syrup that wasn't cooked long enough. Under-cooked syrup could sour if it wasn't cooked hot enough. Wouldn't keep. Amos Reed had to live with himself.

Hugh saw the movement as he drove down the gravel road from Amos's place. At first he thought it was a rotting limb hanging down, a deadman, the locals called it. Swinging in the breeze. He turned toward it and caught the slimmest of shadows as the movement stopped, disappeared.

He studied the distance, the raw, naked, leafless woods. He stopped the car, the wheels crunching the gravel slower and slower until the grinding stopped in the quiet woods. He waited.

The man couldn't wait. He edged himself around the trunk, moving the distance, and Hugh caught him. "Hey!" he shouted.

The man jerked back behind the tree.

Hugh opened the door. "Hey!"

The man stayed put.

Hugh walked across the road and stepped into the spongy, spring woodland, making advancing noise. He kept his eyes on the target tree in the peripheral clutter of the others and eased forward, thinking possibilities. Rifle. Handgun. Threat. Exposure.

The man sprinted from the tree trunk and headed straight back from the road, deeper into the woods. He ran in spastic flicks of his arms and legs, jumping overfallen logs, half-slipping in the mud.

Hugh shouted again, and this time the man looked back over his shoulder, mouth open, eyes white. It was too far to be sure, but it looked like Larry Sedgwick.

10

Stolen waters are sweet.
—Proverbs

IT WAS LARRY. He ran like a fox-chased rabbit, turning and twisting and frantic. He shoved branches out of the way, grabbed tree trunks, gaped at the pursuing hunter behind him. He ran onto the old logging road and stretched his long legs like a newborn giraffe.

"Larry! It's me! Hugh!"

Larry kept running and gaping back over his shoulder.

"Stop, Larry! It's all right!"

The two of them ran down the high center-ridge of the road, but it was Larry who kept half-stumbling on the slippery rocks.

"It's all right, Larry!"

Finally, he stopped and turned around, backing step-by-step away as Hugh, too, stopped running and walked toward him.

"Are you mad at me?" Larry asked, his hands rubbing his chest in circles over each other. "Are you mad at me?"

"No, Larry, I'm not mad at you."

"Yes, you are, you are!"

"I'm not, Larry, not at all. I just wanted to know who that was I saw. You were hiding behind the tree. What were you doing there?"

"I wasn't hiding. You're mad at me," he said, and then

stretched his mouth back, exposing his teeth, breathing heavy from the running.

"What were you doing there?"

"I wasn't hiding."

"Then why did you run away?"

"Amos was making syrup. I was watching Amos making syrup, and Rita was there and you came. Then you left and so I was just watching. You're mad at me."

"Why didn't you just come in? Amos would have let you do some sugaring. I thought you liked Amos."

"I do," Larry said, exposing his teeth again, widening his eyes, his hands still revolving on his chest. "Amos taught me how to sugar. I like to sugar. He teaches me lots of things. He teaches me how to split wood and how to shoot his rifle. He teaches me all those things."

"His rifle?"

Larry bobbed his head. He held up his arms in mock stance of holding a rifle; his fingers curled at odds with each other. "You're mad at me because I saw who shot a rifle at you. People get mad at me for watching all the time, but I see things people shouldn't do and then I tell them I'm going to tell somebody and they get madder and madder and madder. They tell me they're going to shoot me with a rifle and I'm going to end up like Benj Carver. He drowned in all that boiling syrup—uaaggghh. People get real mad at me."

"Wait a minute, Larry. Did you see who shot at me? Where did you see that?"

"They shot at you in your window. I saw them. Your window went all exploding and it went all over the place."

"Who's they, Larry?"

"I saw him. You're mad at me because I was watching you through the window, but I couldn't help. I was just walking out there at night and then I wasn't really watching you but then I saw him with the rifle and it went loud." He put his hands over his ears, his eyes turning upward like a puppy dog's.

"Who was it, Larry?"

"I have to go because I have to send my mother a book, it's about God, and she's going to get mad at me if I don't do it right now, she told me that, I have to go right now, right now!" He bared his teeth in his humorless smile.

"I'm not mad at you, Larry," Hugh said with a softer tone. "It's just that I'm interested in knowing who shot the rifle at me. You can understand that, can't you?"

Larry bobbed his head.

"Do you remember who it was?"

"Nobody."

"It had to be somebody, Larry. Somebody had to shoot the rifle or it wouldn't have gone off and broken my window."

"He ran away. It was too dark. It wasn't anybody because I couldn't see anybody."

"You didn't see anybody?"

"He fell down."

"You saw him fall?"

"He made noise way over there but he ran away. You're mad at me. I have to go because my mother told me to send the book right now, she told me, she told me."

"All right, Larry. You better do that."

"She told me."

"Maybe we can talk about it later."

"People get mad at me when I see things."

Janice called and Hugh went right over. She brewed some camomile tea and they sat at the table by the window. "It's my father," she said. "I'm still worried about him. I wish you could do something to get him away from his place for a while."

It was the shot through the sugarhouse window. Amos could have been inside, not Rita, and blood had priority. "He's doing all right," Hugh said.

"Something's bad going on, Hugh, and it's all happening around my father. It's terrible."

"I know it is."

"Will you talk with him?"

"Sure, of course."

"Just try to get him to go away for a while."

"Where? Besides, you know he won't leave while the sap's still running."

"He'll listen to you."

Hugh smiled.

"He *will*."

"Janice, you know as well as I do that he hardly listens to himself, let alone me."

"Let alone *me*."

"But I'll talk to him."

She reached over and covered his hand with hers. "It's worth a try. I know he's stubborn. I just don't want anything to happen to him."

"Nothing's going to happen to him."

She stood up, walked to the mantle, and brought back a framed photograph. "Can you believe this?" she said, handing it to Hugh. "Twenty years ago and he looks the same. Look at that jaw. Nobody's going to talk him into anything."

"Out by the same sugarhouse."

"It is. The only thing different is that the trees are bigger now. Isn't that typical?"

Hugh liked her green eyes all right, but she smelled good, too, up close. Auburn hair, olive-lush skin. She had full Reed lips and a jawline like Amos's. She was his as plain as rain, and the right sex, too.

"Want some more?"

He nodded and watched her move to the kitchen counter. Jeans. Dark red and burgundy cowboy plaid shirt with gold thread running through it for a touch of glitter. Perfect. "I saw Larry today," he said, making the tone a bit too casual and deliberate.

"Oh? Where?"

"Out by Amos's."

"Dad showed him how to sugar once."

"I know. He tells me that practically every time I see him. He likes Amos."

"Larry would be better if he had somebody like Dad, only his own age. Do you know what I mean?"

"I do. Has Amos ever showed Larry how to use a rifle?"

Janice turned to look over her shoulder at Hugh, her eyes puzzled. "No, he wouldn't do that. Why?"

Hugh shrugged. "I was just wondering."

"No, why, Hugh?"

"Oh, Larry was saying how much he liked Amos and Amos taught him how to sugar and split wood and this and that. Then he said Amos taught him how to use a rifle, too."

Janice shook her head. "No, that wouldn't be Dad. He wouldn't do that with Larry."

"I didn't think so."

Janice finished pouring the tea and brought the cups to the table. "I don't know why he said that."

"Well, you know Larry."

She smiled and nodded. "What else did he say?"

Hugh stalled and took a sip, debating whether to tell her about the shot through his window, what Larry said about seeing somebody in the dark, about Larry prowling around at night. Janice lived alone. She would not want to know that Larry Sedgwick prowled around at night looking in windows and standing in the shadows in the woods. "Oh, not much," he said, clicking the cup down. "We were talking and all of a sudden he said he had to go send his mother a book."

Janice smiled.

"What?"

"His mother died years ago."

Hugh stared at her.

"You didn't know that?"

"No."

"Some awful thing. She fell down the basement stairs."

Janice said something else, but Hugh didn't hear it. He traced his conversations since he was shot at and could think of no one he had told; he said nothing to anyone. Then Larry must have seen it happen; he didn't hear it from somebody else, unless he heard it from the one who fired the shot. That was ridiculous. Reality faded in and out for Larry, but even if his mother told him to send her a book, he still could not have known about the shot unless he was there watching, an accident of time and place, a chance meeting in the thick shadows.

"She was pretty old."

"Who?"

"Larry's mother," Janice said, cocking her head, questioning Hugh's attention.

"You have gorgeous eyes."

She smiled.

He followed her to the sink, which he leaned against while she washed the cups, cleaned the tea pot, sponged the sink. He took the dishtowel and dried the cups.

"Just talk to Dad, will you, Hugh? It won't do any good, I know, but it'll make me feel better."

"He says that since the war he doesn't get scared getting shot at anymore. What do you say to that?"

"Oh, he's scared."

Hugh nodded.

"Was Dad showing Larry how to do more about sugaring?"

"No, not really."

Janice waited.

"Well, he was just watching the sugarhouse from the woods someplace. I just happened to see him on the way out. I thought it was somebody else. Actually, I didn't know who it was at first. Then he started to run. He was scared, I guess, but he stopped and we talked."

"What was he doing out there?"

"You know Larry."

"I know, but if all this hadn't been happening I wouldn't give it a second thought."

"I talked to him. It was all right. And I'll talk to Amos."

Janice smiled and touched his hand again.

She was staying close, and those green eyes, too. She had a streak of extremes in her, the allure of inner woman mixed with the outer manly paraphernalia. Cowboy woman. Snug jeans encasing female body. The ambivalence of millennia—woman and female, the madness of men. How much was she Janice, how much Woman?

He held her look, and then he held her hand. He leaned to kiss her and she waited.

The curse of copdom. He should never have been a cop. Once a cop always a cop. The legal terms were inclination and opportunity. God Almighty knew that he had the inclination. Inclination? Lust! Friendly, caring, loving lust. Here he was inclining. Puns! Never read books. Don't think. Don't think about thinking. Opportunity? *Here* was opportunity. Permission granted, signed Green Eyes. Here indeed was opportunity, and his gut was beginning to go. The heart beat quickening, the lungs tightening. Woman or Janice? Janice or Woman? What ancient absurdities rule our lives.

He kissed her, and her head fell back with so much soft

surrender and acceptance and drowning power that he leaned more over her to keep kissing her. It was startling, wonderful, ingenuously corroborating. He was *wanted.*

He kissed her with enwrapping arms until they parted on a mutual flush of expectations. They smiled at each other. Then Hugh looked down at her blouse and very carefully, very slowly, gently, unbuttoned the top button.

Janice kept her hands on his waist and watched his hands. "You have gorgeous hands," she said. Half jest, half true, wholly invitational.

Hugh kissed her momentarily on her lips, just enough for her to part them for more, disappointed. Then he kissed her on her neck as she leaned her head to the side to help him help her. He unbuttoned the second button very carefully, very slowly, gently, and with the back of his hand brushed back the edge of her blouse, exposing the first rise of her breast.

He looked up and she looked up and they smiled like grown-up man and woman knowing oh so well that they were male and female and that was how the world worked. Let it happen, it was going fine, let's proceed to the point of no return.

He looked down again and she, too. He *had* to kiss her again. So he leaned to her lips and she raised them, wet and parting. They kissed deeply and pressed against each other, the half-opened blouse more a seduction of imagination, a stimulating presence, a reminder than what it really exposed.

They looked at each other again, smiling, enjoying this ladder on themselves, sort of laughing at themselves but not enough to stop it. They looked down at his hands again as he unbuttoned the third button, pushed the blouse aside, this time to see the signs of quickening in Janice's breath.

The phone rang.

Hugh ignored it and moved his hand along the top of her breast, easing inside her bra to slide his hand around her.

"Oh," Janice moaned, the moan of interruption, realertness, disappointment.

He leaned to kiss her again on her neck; the phone rang.

It was impossible to undress a woman when the goddamn phone was ringing. The ring was an all-seeing eye, tyrannous disturber of benevolent surrender, an outrageous shatterer, outrageous. He fought the inevitable with his controlled, persuasive, lingering, hopeful calm and caresses, but they were not persuasive enough.

Janice looked up and with pleading green eyes that signaled the impossibility of sharing his omnipotent tolerance, she buttoned her blouse. The phone rang. Hugh cursed. Ah, but the eyes had tomorrow in them.

11

Evil events from evil causes spring.

—Aristophanes

THE NEXT MORNING Hugh called Proctor Hammond to see what he could find out about the Unger part of Perley & Unger. That afternoon Proctor called back and said, "Easy."

"Well?"

"What do you want to know?"

"Who is he? What's he do? All you know."

"Quint, all I know is not what you want. That would take longer than you're willing to spend. You would get bored. You would miss the point. You would quickly deteriorate from enjoyment to irritation and hang up right in the middle of one of my sentences. You would—"

"I got it, Proctor."

"See."

"Yes, I interrupted you in the middle of one of your sentences. I see, Proctor. Now about Unger."

"The trouble with you, Quint, is a certain laxity in the application of your lofty education. I've been thinking. I trust that you dug out the bullet that that loony up there in the wilds shot through your window and that you sent it to ballistics."

"No."

"You didn't dig out the bullet."

"I did."

"You didn't send it to ballistics."

"I don't want anyone to know about it yet. But some-body does," he said and told Proctor about Larry.

"You've thought about the fact that if Larry didn't see who the assassin was, at least he *says* so, you must have thought of the reverse: The assassin saw Larry."

Hugh said nothing.

"You didn't think of that. I would suggest, Quint, that you get a play-by-play account of this little merry tale of murder and see if this Larry is in any danger. It's an old law of physics that I apply to all aspects of sociopolitical life: For every action there's a reaction. Look both ways before crossing the street. What goes up must come down. If Larry saw someone, someone might have seen Larry."

"Point taken."

"Larry could get to be a worrisome ingredient for this murdering loony in your treacherous woods, for which I would give nothing for the privilege to ignore."

"You are such a city boy, Proctor."

"Nobody has shot at me, Quint."

"Right, Proctor."

"Nobody has killed any of my neighbors, Quint."

"Right, Proctor, right. Now what about Unger?"

"Arthur Unger of Henry Perley and Arthur Unger is an ordinary, all-American, thieving entrepreneurial capitalist given sanction by our national mores to gather as much profit in building and construction as is humanly possible. My sources tell me *he* has sources and resources in state planning offices, building permit divisions, tax assessing departments, all the usual conduits to capitalistic excess. He transforms emptiness into marine sites, builds piers and boat harbors, sets up tourist attractions in harbors to get both the land crowd and the water people. He gets them coming and going, so to speak. He built the Hatter's Island project."

"I know that place."

"And lots more. He likes water. He's never been

convicted of fraud or safe-construction violations, but he's been to court. He has wife number three, two big kids, one on deep drugs, three houses—monuments to his wives, I presume—backs any politician, *local* politicians, of course, who reveals the slightest puerile interest in concrete blocks. He's a big deal if you favor concrete, but then we all know that you like wood."

"Ever use pencils, Proctor?"

"I'm saving an interesting little subterranean fact for last. You may not apply the rubber band principle to this tidbit of curious information, but I would if I were in your place."

"What are you talking about, Proctor?"

"I'm talking about the rubber band principle of elongation. Nobody knows anything about rubber bands. Rubber bands are an omnipresent feature of our society, and nobody knows a damn thing about them."

"Maybe they don't care."

"We manufacture twenty million pounds of rubber bands a year in this country, twenty *million* pounds. Vulcanization mixes rubber and sulfur under heat, and that keeps the rubber elastic."

"I know, Proctor. Goodyear did it."

"And you know the year, too, of course."

"Hell, no."

"1839."

"Christ, Proctor."

"Get U.S. Postal Service rubber bands. Save them. They're the best because rubber band makers . . ."

"Rubber band makers?"

". . . have to come up to Postal Service standards, which is, *Quint*, a 700 percent elongation. This means that a one-inch rubber band must stretch seven inches without breaking or tearing."

"Very interesting, Proctor."

"Now when I tell you this next little fact about Arthur Unger, you'll thank me for the rubber band principle. I found out from another source, in an undisclosed tax-related agency, shall we say, that Arthur Unger has several cousins."

"Not too interesting."

"What ignited *my* interest was that one of these cousins lives in Lyme." Proctor paused. "I do think I have your attention."

"I'm listening."

"David Tefler."

"Judas."

"Sounds better than I thought."

"He's the real-estate agent that got strangled."

"Ah, more threads are showing, but logically, it proves nothing. Here's where the rubber band principle works. One-to-one relationships mean nothing. Unger of Perley and Unger is a cousin of David Tefler of Lyme. That's as far as it goes. But if you stretch your imagination about 700 percent, you'll have more related possibilities to play with. Rubber bands encompass more when they're stretched. That's the rubber band principle, Quint. Don't get shot."

The phone rang as soon as Hugh hung up. "I've been trying to get you," Rita said, her voice quick and serious.

"I've been on the phone."

"I know. I don't know how to put this, but Amos and I found someone dead. Stabbed."

He thought of Larry Sedgwick and said nothing. It wasn't Larry or she would have said so; she knew him. "Who, Rita?"

"We don't know. We were going over to Benj's place to get some cordwood, and there he was."

"Did you call the Chief?"

"Yes, but I thought you'd want to know."

"I'll be right over. Amos all right?"

"He's all right."

"You'll be at Benj's?"

"Right."

When Hugh pulled into Benj Carver's driveway, he parked alongside the Chief's patrol car. He got out, walked by the side of the house, and saw Rita, Amos, and the Chief standing by the sugarhouse in the back. They turned toward him, said nothing as he approached, and then they all looked at the body.

The man was draped facedown over the heap of logs. He lay there, spread-eagled in a jagged curve, his arms cocked in a scarecrow angle, his legs out of sync with life. A grooved, crescentlike piece of metal stuck out his back. His face was cut where he had fallen against the wood. He was long dead.

"What is that?" Hugh finally asked.

"That's what you know," Amos said. "That's a tap. Collects sap. You jam it into the tree, you hang the bucket on it, and you get the sap when it drips out. Makes a good knife, don't it?"

The Chief opened his hands. "Well, anybody know him?"

"I never seen him before," Amos said, pouting in defense. "That's why you think I killed him, don't ya?"

"I never said that, Amos," the Chief said. "All I said was, Does anybody know him. I've never seen him around here. Maybe you people have."

"I told you. I never saw him before this. Look at him, dead there like some lazy know-nothing. He's in the right place, all right, Benj Carver's place."

"Come on, Amos," Rita said.

"Come on where?"

Rita sighed and turned to the Chief. "We came over to get some firewood and there he was," she said and pointed to the man.

"What's the use of having all this wood here and nobody *using* it," Amos shouted. "Benj never used it. Never used it *right*. So that's what happened. You don't believe me, do you?"

"I believe you," the Chief said. "Why not?"

"That's what I say."

They looked at the body again. The man was average build. Green outdoor workpants, Maine boots for the mud season, L. L. Bean gray wool shirt-jacket. The metal tap must have been sharpened to penetrate the thick cloth and plunge deep enough into his back to kill him with one blow. No other stab wound was visible. He could have been stabbed by surprise, which was hard to do up close in the woods, or maybe by somebody the man knew and got it when he turned his back.

"Did you hear anything?" the Chief asked.

"Hell, no," Amos shouted. "What do you mean hear anything? We're *working*. We're sugaring and you ask us if we hear anything. What do you mean hear anything?"

"Amos, I just want to know if anybody heard anything. Maybe there was a scuffle, maybe some shouting, some argument, how do I know? That's what I want to find out."

"Well, find out from somebody else."

"No," Rita said, intervening, "we didn't hear anything. We came over and there he was. I don't mind telling you, I didn't like seeing him there."

"Maybe he has some identification," Hugh said to the Chief.

"Yeah, ever think of that?" Amos shouted.

The Chief ignored him and said to Hugh, "I didn't want to disturb the body. I wanted to get some photos of him just where he is."

"Just take his wallet out, why the hell can't you do that?" Amos shouted. "You don't even have to turn him over, can't you see that?"

"I suppose so," the Chief said and reached inside the man's back pocket. He removed the wallet with quick jerks of his hand and opened it to the driver's license.

"Well?" Amos shouted.

"Bill Kanin."

"Never heard of him."

"Boston address."

"What's he doing up here?" Amos said.

"What's he doing on Benj's land is what I'd like to know," Rita said.

"What about a car?" Hugh asked. "Anybody see it? He must have one around here, unless he walked all the way in from town."

"Bostons don't walk," Amos said.

" 'Course, we just walked through the woods here," Rita said. "We couldn't see anything even if there was one. You didn't see one?"

"No," Hugh said.

"Well, did *you?*" Amos asked the Chief.

"You interrogating me, Amos?"

"The man's dead in here and he's Boston and he didn't hitchhike up here to get stabbed next to my place. Do you figure that? He's got a car someplace. You drove up. You see anything?"

"I didn't see a car, Amos."

"Didn't think so."

The Chief flipped systematically through the card folders in the wallet.

"Well, there's a car here someplace," Amos went on. "The dead man's car, whatever his name is. Was. Bill Kanin. Never heard of him. How do you think he got here? I know that much and I ain't been to a police *school.*"

"We'll look for it," the Chief said. "We'll find it."

"He could be visiting someone up here," Hugh said. "Left his car someplace and just started walking."

"You get stabbed in the *back* for doing something like that up here, you know that, don't you?" Amos said. "Maybe Benj did."

"Amos," Rita said.

"Could be," the Chief said to Hugh.

"He's trespassing, ain't he?" Amos said.

"It's not his land, if that's what you mean?" the Chief said, still sorting through the wallet, counting the bills.

"First it's Davy, and then it's Benj, now it's this one, whoever the hell he is," Amos shouted. "Next it's going to be whoever the hell it's going to be. They shot my window out, you know. Shot out the sugarhouse. They almost killed Rita, didn't they?"

Rita nodded.

"Maybe he did it. Maybe he shot it out, ever think of that?"

The Chief looked up with tired eyes. "Then why's he dead?"

"Don't ask me, I'm no COP," Amos shouted. "Figure it out. You got the badge. The badge makes you smart, that's what they say. Plenty of *tax* money for that badge."

"How long do you figure he's been dead," Hugh asked the Chief, trying to deflect the harangue.

"I'm no medical examiner."

"We all know that," Amos shouted.

"But I'd say probably some time now. Six, seven hours. Probably more. They got a schedule for rigor mortis all worked out. They'll know."

"Sure they will," Amos said and pointed to the man. "Look at him. Maybe somebody thought he was a maple tree and stuck it in him."

"Amos!" Rita said.

"City people don't know nothing, you know. Get them up here and they'll do anything. I seen one plant a garden first warm week in March. Got cold again and killed it. He could be doing anything like that up here."

"Don't think so," the Chief said, still looking at the wallet.

"You found something," Hugh said.

"Business card. He's a surveyor."

12

Murder will out.
—Chaucer

THE TOWN CLERK'S office was in the usual state of benign omnipotence when Hugh walked in and saw Sarah Baylord officiating from her corner desk. She looked up and smiled with gentle, elderly, camouflaged almightiness, obviously content in her hoary ability to disseminate favors and information. The top of her desk was crowded but neatly arranged; she was tallying overdue property tax payments. Even though the statement for the town report was never due until the end of the year, Sarah Baylord kept up-to-date. Sarah Baylord knew at all times who the dirty-rat delinquents were.

"They had a fire up at Fletcher's," she said before Hugh opened his mouth. "This morning. Chimney fire, all that wood burning through winter and nobody cleans out the creosote. I told Betsy a hundred times if I told her once, 'Better clean out the chimney this year, Betsy, or you'll have a fire, don't you know.' So now they had a fire."

"Nobody hurt, I hope."

"The chimney got hurt," she said, her sweet, belying voice matching the grandmotherly shake of her head, "but the rest just got scared. Petey got there first. He's always there first, you know. He was in my fourth grade when I taught school. I taught school, did you know that?"

Of course, she taught school.

"That's why we've got the best volunteer fire department in the state," she said. "I know why you're here."

"Why, Sarah?"

"Because of that killing." She tilted her head down, raised her eyebrows, nodded with a knowing smile.

"You're too fast for me, Sarah."

"I know."

"You heard that on the radio, too?"

"I know the codes. I know the Chief, too. Terrible thing. I don't know what this town is coming to. Killings and shootings. It's like what I watch on TV. You want to know about Bill Kanin, don't you?"

Hugh smiled. "You even know his name."

"He came in here all right. I know a stranger when I see one. 'Course, I don't let on too much. You have to treat everybody the same in this office, but he was a stranger all right. Nice looking young man. I always let strangers think they're charming me. I've seen a few years, you know. And I've known a few men in my time, I know about them. Now I don't say that in the Biblical sense, you understand, but maybe I mean it that way, too. You never know what old ladies have seen and done, do you? People think little old ladies have always been little old ladies."

"Not you, Sarah, never."

She winked and smiled. Then she said, because Hugh was biding his time, "Oh, Bill Kanin was in here all right. He came in, and he didn't fool me. He was chatting about this and that and then he said he'd like to look at the tax map. I asked him which section and he told me. Then he looked at this and that and I asked him a few questions. I could see he was looking at the property lines. I made a pretty good guess."

"Of what?"

"You know what," she said. She knitted concerned

eyebrows together and asked, "Don't you want to sit down?"

"No, not right now."

"In a hurry, aren't you? I can tell. You can tell a lot about people just sitting in this chair. People don't think so, but you can."

"*You* can."

She smiled, her watery blue eyes not missing a twitch. "Too bad you weren't in my class."

"I'd probably have given you a hard time, Sarah. I'm still trying to figure out what to do when I grow up."

"I know all about you, Hugh."

"That's what unnerves me, Sarah."

"So this Bill Kanin, a stranger coming into Lyme, well, I figured what he was up to. I made a good guess at it. Then when I heard he was killed out there, my guess was right."

Hugh waited.

"He was a surveyor all right," she said, nodding.

"The Chief found that in his identification."

"I know, I heard. You want to know something else, don't you?"

"Whatever you know."

"I asked him about this and that and I figured who hired him, who he was working for," she said. She swiveled in her squeaky chair and tapped the delinquent taxpayer list. "You know who I'm talking about. I told you about him. He came in here once and thought he knew more than I did. You know him. You know this Henry Perley."

Chances were always good that Amos was outside someplace. So Hugh found him to the side of the sugarhouse splitting logs and stacking them in long neat rows. Methodically. He was in no hurry because he had plenty of split wood already. It was a matter of preparation. It was doing something outdoors, where he belonged, as long as he could keep awake and warm.

Hugh and Amos went through their routine until Hugh slipped in the message. "Amos," he said, "I've been thinking. Why don't you shut down the sugarhouse, the sap's just about through running anyhow, and go south for a visit or something. Take some time off. You've been working too hard. It'd be a perfect time, and besides, you can let this whole shooting mess blow over in the meantime."

"South?" he shouted.

"Well, anywhere really."

"You mean Africa? How 'bout Africa?"

"You know what I mean."

"*Mexico.*"

"I'm worried about you."

"Nobody's shooting me, and nothing's going to blow over me. And don't give me that baloney about being worried about me. I know who sent you up here to weasel me. You weren't doing the thinking."

Hugh stared at the chunky set jaws and dagger eyes, heard the words blasting out the grizzled old mouth. He felt failure loom ahead as sure as B followed A, but duty beckoned, a promise made was a debt unpaid and all that other philosophical crap, and he knew he was going to cower back to Janice and report the predictable inevitable: Amos was a goddamn stubborn cuss and if he gets his head blown off it's his own goddamn fault.

"Janice sent you, *admit* it."

"All right, Amos, Janice sent me."

"Ha! I knew she made you. You sure wouldn't do it yourself. You'd like to see me get my head blown off, wouldn't you? See, you're laughing."

"Not at that, Amos."

"You and the Chief."

"Janice doesn't like you staying here alone."

"Why not? Been doing it for years."

"Not with these killings going on."

"What's she worried about? *She's* staying alone. Or is she? You moving in there?"

"Hell, no, Amos. What do you think?"

"I know what's going on," Amos said and set a log on its edge. Before raising the two-handed axe over his head and slicing the log in two with one whack, he said, "You don't fool me."

"Who's fooling you, Amos? She's your daughter."

"Don't forget it!" he shouted. "And don't tell me anything about it, you hear?"

"What?"

"You know what I'm talking about."

"Hell, Amos."

Amos kicked the logs out of the way. "She's a woman, you know."

"She's an attractive young woman, Amos."

"SEE!"

Hugh cocked his head back at the thunder.

"Don't tell me about it!"

"You're the one talking about her, Amos."

"That's different. I don't want YOU talking about her. She's modern, you know. Now she wants me to give up this place."

"She doesn't want that. She just wants you to get away for a while, take a break. It's not right for you staying around here with all this happening. She's just offering a suggestion."

"She can't weasel me and she thinks you can. That's what she knows."

"Think about it."

"Everybody's making me offers. I'm a church?"

"They like you."

"Ha. They want this place."

"Who?"

"Davy made me an offer, for one."

Hugh stared at Amos's horseshoe mouth and glowering eyebrows. "Davy Tefler?"

"You heard."

"He was making you an offer to buy your place for someone else?" Hugh asked, correcting Amos. "As a real estate agent?"

"People can't hear what's said anymore. I said, Davy made me an offer. Not somebody else. Davy."

"What'd you say?"

"What do you think I said?"

Hugh asked Rita to come in and sit down. She came in all right, but she paced back and forth like a tigress with a triumph in her jowls. Her eyes were lighted up in the leathery face, her lean frame stalking the room. Transmogrify her to Alexander the Great (Joan of Arc was out of the question) and she'd be carried on her warriors' shields. As it was, Rita Dinsmore announced with vengeful joy that she knew who hired Bill Kanin, the surveyor.

"I know," Hugh said, restraining himself to an honorable show of counter joy.

"You know?"

He nodded. "Perley."

"Right, Perley!" she said, jabbing her stiff ten fingers at him, her palms up, her hungry eyes flaring. "So that's it!"

"What do you mean that's it?"

"I mean," she said, impatiently searching the word, "now we know what he's up to. We know what's going on here."

"We know that the man who got killed was a surveyor. We don't even know if he was up here surveying."

"He's not up here walking in Amos's woods for nothing. Come on, Hugh. I'll say it right out. It's murder for big money. Perley is setting it up, and to do that he has to get rid of people that are in the way. You think I'm jumping to conclusions, but, Hugh, the facts are there, they're pointing straight at that Perley thug."

He stepped to the side window, leaned against the framing, and glanced at the woods; it was a new habit. "Let's put it this way. It doesn't make sense in itself, but the coincidences conjure some possibilities."

"Let's put it *this* way. Perley is hooked up with Fratacelli, and Perley hired Kanin to do a survey job. He didn't hire Kanin to pick blueberries, he hired him for a survey. You put Fratacelli with Kanin together and you get some slash and burn mayhem up around here, I'm telling you, Hugh. That's what it is. They're going to bulldoze the place and they're going to lay asphalt from here to kingdom come. I'm telling you, that's it."

"Perley lives here. He's not going to pave it."

"Perley I know. I know what he is. I know the kind. They're two-legged wallets. They'll go where the dollar bills are. They don't give a damn about the woods. Live here? Are you serious? He'll pave it over and move away. He'll build it and move."

"What're you talking about, Rita?"

"I'm talking about condominiums, that's what I'm talking about. Condominiums!"

Hugh pursed his lips. Disguise: He was destroying a smile. Never smile at Rita unless she smiled first. Condominiums was one of her buzzwords, like toxic waste, acid rain, extinction, nuclear winter, meltdown. Condominiums ignited the eyes, and Rita's eyes were nothing to fuss with.

"I'm talking about condominiums, that's what I'm talking about. Condominiums!"

Hugh pursed his lips. Disguise: He was destroying a smile. Never smile at Rita unless she smiled first. Condominiums was one of her buzzwords, like toxic waste, acid rain, extinction, nuclear winter, meltdown. Condominiums ignited the eyes, and Rita's eyes were nothing to fuss with.

"I'm talking about condominiums," she repeated. "He's surveying for condominiums, and Fratacelli's in with him. In fact, that goddamn Fratacelli is probably the one who got him up to it. They're in it together. They'll bulldoze the trees, stuff some condos in there, asphalt the rest of it, and then you know what?"

When she didn't continue, Hugh said, "What?"

"They'll squeeze the state to put in an interstate. That's what happens. Condos and interstates. This place'll be right on some gigantic interstate because that's what they're up to, I know it."

"Rita," Hugh said, hands in supplication, "there aren't enough people for an interstate. How can they justify that?"

She was ready for it. "That's the mistake. Interstates don't come *after* the people, they come *before* them. Population follows interstates, not precedes them. What do you think the railroads did? Stick a railroad across the empty West and then the people come and fill it up. Stick an interstate through here, and then they come with their strip malls and fast food junk and more condominiums. That's the way it works. It doesn't work any other way. Because some fat-assed earth killer like Fratacelli hooks up with some greedy nail-pounder like Perley and what do you get, you get what *they* want, not what you want, because nobody can see anything in front of their stubby little noses, and when they do it's too late, too late!"

Hugh remembered the school board meeting when Rita stood up and ranted and raved about the stupidity of shortsighted people who didn't know a whit about the interdependence of nature and why shouldn't it be taught in the third grade anyway. The people in the chairs squirmed and bobbed fingers on their knees; the board stared at her. She was supposed to be supporting the idea that the board had agreed upon in the first place, but style smothered substance and the board got so irritated that it postponed the decision until the next meeting.

"Don't you see, Hugh? They want the lake. It's the purest lake water in the state—6.2 reading out of 7. That's why they're surveying it. Condominiums. The land is worth Fort Knox. Benj is out of the way. Benj's property is between Perley's and Amos's, and Amos's is right on the shore. They're aiming to grab the whole batch so they can have direct access to the water. Piers, speedboat races, all that stuff. That's the way Fratacelli works, and Perley is working for him."

"You forget," Hugh said, making stop signs of his hands. "Kanin was killed. You don't hire a surveyor and then kill him."

"Perley does. Fratacelli does."

"It doesn't make sense."

"Kanin was found on Amos's property."

"So?"

"So Perley killed him to blame Amos."

13

By honest means, if you can, but by any means make money.

—Horace

THE TIME CAME to check out Henry Perley, so Hugh drove to the new gray-painted slat-board house with the black-tarred driveway decorated with the white Cadillac.

He pushed the white button in the brass enclosure beneath the shiny brass porch light. An old-time Lyme house this was not. He had fabricated some involved stream of dialogue and convoluted scene to make himself plausible and to get past the front door. Waste of time. Instead of big Henry, his wife, Millicent, answered the door.

The outside signaled the inside: white shag rug, glass and brass cocktail table, *Connoisseur* magazine and others of the ilk displayed cover up, of course. The walls were papered with hotel neutral beige, two giant scallop-shell lamps were stationed on both sides of the mammoth three-section sofa. The "entertainment" corner glistened with silver control panels in, of course, the latest digital astronaut mode—video recorders, stereo phonograph and radio, mammoth color television (the rooftop aerial matched the size). It was the kind of summer home one expected of indoor people.

He asked if Henry was available, and Millicent said that he'd be right out, would Hugh like something to drink. No, thank you. She was a smiling, short-haired matron of pale, thin skin and mid-day Bostonian clothes—yellow and red print dress with blouse-style collar. Hazel eyes. Bright, old-style red lipstick just in case a visitor arrived.

Henry walked in, his hands stretched in greeting. The two men introduced themselves, shook hands, said nothing about seeing each other in Benj's sugarhouse or when Hugh was birdwatching, so to speak. Perley's grip was solid, contractorlike. Full of hammers and nails.

"Ask Mr. Quint to sit down, Henry," Millicent said.

"It's Hugh, please."

She smiled and glanced at Henry who said, "Yes, sit down, sit down. What brings you here?"

Hugh sank in the fluffed, rose cushion chair and felt himself awash in the jarring hospitality, the startling smiles and recognition in Perley. What happened to the mood of trespass?

"Isn't it terrible about that killing?" Millicent asked, exposing what the two men were ignoring, anticipating what the visit was all about in the first place.

"Yes, terrible," Hugh said, nodding, agreeing, being indebted. "Actually, that's what I was wondering about."

"Oh?" Perley said, but the sense of challenge was totally absent, as if he, too, were immersed in basic curiosity.

"And he was such a nice man," Millicent said. "Oh, dear. And it happened so close to here. It's just so frightening. I don't know what to think. This has always been such a quiet place, and safe, too. I just don't know what to think."

"I don't blame you," Hugh said.

"You're an interested party, I take it," Perley said, smiling, voice well modulated. But the eyes: so well focused.

"Well, of course, anyone living in Lyme would be interested," Hugh said, "it's that kind of town."

"Oh, of course," Millicent said, her hand at her breast.

"A little more interested than that, I take it," Perley said, nodding a camaraderie secret.

"The Chief is busy and, well, you know small towns, he asked me to help him out."

"Isn't that nice?" Millicent said.

Hugh nodded to her and turned to Perley. "The Chief wanted to make sure that the rumor was right. That you hired Bill Kanin."

Perley glanced at Millicent for interrupting him as she said, "Oh, yes, we did hire him. I even served him lunch that day. He was so nice."

Then Perley said, with ever pleasant assurance, "It was a little surveying job. You know he was a surveyor, I take it."

Hugh nodded. "We found out. What exactly did you want him to do?"

"Just a little surveying job," Perley said.

"We just wanted him to survey our property lines," Millicent said, interrupting again, drawing Perley's smiling but tolerant stare. "I don't know who would do such a thing. It makes me think we're somewhere else."

Perley said, "Do you have any idea who it was?"

"Some," Hugh said, feeling the exuberance of using such an unintended but gratuitous opportunity to exchange contingencies.

"And with all these other killings," Millicent said, while her husband and Hugh lingered watchful eyes on each other in such charming company. "Do you think it's all connected?"

"It may be, Mrs. Perley," Hugh said.

"Oh, Millicent, please."

Hugh smiled appreciation. "Everything is connected

in unusual ways. Surprising ways. You never know, do you? Now I never knew that"—he turned to Perley—"your partner was a cousin to Davy Tefler."

"Arthur?" Millicent said with no hint that Hugh had just dropped a bomb of a revelation into the conversation. "Oh, yes, that's how we knew about this nice town."

"You never know, do you?" Perley said.

"We were so upset about Davy. We just don't know what to think. He was such a nice young man. And to find him like that, well, I just don't know. It was terrible."

"It was," Hugh said.

"Everybody has cousins," Perley said. "Yes, it was unfortunate what happened."

"Now Henry may not have got along with Davy too much on everything," Millicent said, adding—undecipherably—"but then you have to remember that Davy and Arthur were cousins, and, after all, Henry is Arthur's partner. Blood is thicker than water, isn't it?"

"Yes, it is," Hugh said, trying to re-cement this fractured idea about blood between partners, and failing. "It all seems so coincidental, doesn't it, Millicent?"

"But that's what connections are," she said. "Everybody is connected to everybody else, well, everybody is connected to somebody, and I know that I run into people connected to me or Henry all the time. It's a small world after all. And here was Davy, who first got us interested in Lyme, poor man, and now all these other connections with all these killings. I just don't know."

"It's very confusing," Hugh said.

"Yes, it is. Now Henry, why don't you offer Mr. Quint . . ."

"Remember, it's Hugh."

". . . Oh, yes, Hugh, why don't you offer him something to drink?"

110

"What would you like?" Perley asked. The teeth showed but the tone was perfunctory, compliant, anticipatory to a negative.

"No, thank you, I have to be going," Hugh said, standing up, drawing them to their feet, too.

"Let me show you what Kanin was going to do for us," Perley said.

"Yes," Millicent said, smiling, "why don't you do that, Henry? You two men go outdoors and I'll fix something in here just in case you change your mind, Hugh."

That was the essence of it and now Hugh had it pegged. Big Henry was the docile jester in Millicent's kingdom of the house. Long ago it must have gone something like this: Millicent one day screamed bloody murder at her ham-headed husband to stick his butt out the door and keep it there where it belonged and leave the house to her. If he didn't like the way she ran it, *he* could run it. He had the rest of the world but this house, goddamn it, was *her* house and if she ever heard another word about it from him she'd scissor off his balls in the middle of the night. It must have worked on Big Henry because, after all, you never knew about short-haired matrons.

The other side of it was that Millicent, the innocent, knew nothing really of what went on with Henry Perley in the outside world. She kept it that way. They had their understanding, clear enough, and it was all confirmed when Perley led Hugh out the door and, without a word, trudged through the brush toward a stone wall sloping down to Benj Carver's place.

Hugh could see the transmogrification take place as Perley marched through the woods. His back straightened, his arms swung with deliberate cadence, his fingers fisted together. He led the way with twig-mangling strides, Puck turned Genghis Khan.

When they reached the wall, Perley halted and, like a six-year-old making pistols of his fingers, pointed to the piled row of gray stones. "That's my property line," he announced. Then, in an abrupt switch he turned face on to Hugh and demanded, "What're you insinuating around here? Coming in here and hooking me up with Kanin and this Davy kid. So what?"

Gone the demure household obedience. Gone the charm. "I just asked a question," Hugh said, surrendering his arms, steadying the stallion.

"I don't hold by this small town shit. I hired this Kanin and it's my business what I hired him for."

"It gets to be big business when he gets killed."

"I can't help that. I told you, I hired him to survey my property. I want to know where my lines are. That's a crime around here? What is it, a federal case or something?"

"I thought that was your line."

"That's it," Perley said, jabbing his gun-hand to the wall again. "I told you."

"So you know."

"I want to know exactly."

"But your deed tells you the lines."

"I *told* you. I want to know exactly. How do I know what mistakes they make. This is small town shit around here, you know."

"Right."

"I don't want mistakes on my property. Especially now."

"What do you mean, now?"

Perley tossed his head toward Benj Carver's. "That guy getting killed. How do I know what's going to happen with his place. Never liked the son-of-a-bitch, anyway."

"And then Kanin."

"Yeah."

"You know," Hugh said, twisting his mouth in su-preme—fake—cogitation, "what I don't understand is how Kanin was killed on Benj Carver's property. He was supposed to be surveying your land."

Perley stared back. "What's that supposed to mean?"

Hugh shrugged.

"How do I know what he was doing there? I told him, 'Listen, survey my place and let me know where the exact lines are.' Ask him, if he wasn't killed. What am I going to tell him to go down there for? I don't give a damn about those old-timers. They're nothing to me. They protect their places like some kind of bank or something. Can't step on a rock of theirs without getting shot. What am I going to tell Kanin to go down there for? Hell."

"That's where he was."

"He went down there to look at the lake. How do I know?"

"Did he do any surveying for you?"

"No. None. Nothing. I bring him up here and he gets it."

"He didn't even start?"

"How do I know? Maybe he took out his tripod and all that shit. I don't know. I didn't hire him to watch him."

"Nobody ever saw it."

"That's my fault?"

"No, I just thought you might know where his equip-ment is." Hugh waited and then made sure: "Do you?"

"Hell, no."

"Kanin wasn't looking over Carver's and Amos's places, was he?"

"Hell, no," Perley said. Then, with hard, defiant eyes staring straight on, he added, "What would he do that for?"

This was enough for Hugh to think about, but when

Larry Sedgwick intercepted him outside the post office an hour later, Hugh saw another link slipping into place. Maybe, depending on whether Larry's synapses were in calm working order.

He was wearing his usual seed cap, and his usual far-stretched smile. He started out saying, "I know something you don't."

"Larry, the whole world knows something I don't know, and that includes you. What is it that you know?"

"You won't believe me," he said, nodding and bobbing, eyes bright with treasure. "I know you won't."

"Sure, I will. Why shouldn't I?"

"People don't believe me. I know they don't believe me. Because when I tell them something, they don't believe me."

"Oh, they probably do, Larry," Hugh said, shuffling through three come-on-catalogs and a notice of a free portable television set if only he came to tour a Lakes Region resort condominium.

"They don't, they don't, I know it."

"You think so?" Hugh asked absently.

"They didn't believe me when I said that I need a friend. They didn't believe me when I told them that, and now they all watch me. But you know what? You know what?"

"What, Larry?"

"I watch *them!*" He laughed his high giggle laugh and nodded like a woodpecker. He stretched his mouth back as far as it would go.

Hugh smiled back. Actually, Larry's exuberant innocence was infectious.

"I do!"

"I know you do, Larry." Hugh stepped away and Larry followed, half-turning as he talked.

"I watch them and I see things they don't see. That's how I know things they don't know. That's how I know things. I watch things and they don't even know I'm watching things. They don't even know that I'm watching *them*."

"They probably don't, Larry."

"Do you think they'll get back at me?"

"I don't think so, Larry."

"I do. They're always trying to get back at me. They think I'm seeing things I shouldn't see."

"Are you?"

His eyes brightened, his eyebrows lifted, his head bobbed. "I like it."

"Well, Larry, I don't think people like being watched."

"Oh, they don't see me. Do you think they do?"

"I don't think so, but you better not let them."

"I never do. That's why I know things that other people don't. That's why I know something you don't."

"What's that, Larry?"

"You'll tell."

"I won't tell anybody. Who's there to tell?"

"Will you tell Amos? You'll tell Amos."

"I won't tell Amos. Why should I?"

"I won't tell you if you tell Amos."

"Is it a secret about Amos?"

"No, no, no, but it's about Benj, and Amos doesn't like Benj. Benj is dead but Amos doesn't like him still."

"I don't know about that, Larry."

"If I tell you, will you tell Amos?"

"I won't tell him that I heard anything from you. How's that, Larry?"

"Promise? Do you promise?"

"I promise."

"Do you know what I know? It's Ernie. Remember Ernie? Do you know Ernie?"

"Ernie Carver?"

Larry nodded and stretched his mouth. "Ernie

Carver! He's Benj's brother. He's here, he's in Lyme. I saw him but he doesn't want anybody to see him. I saw him."

"Are you sure, Larry?" Hugh asked, squinting to squeeze out the truth.

Larry bobbed his head. "He has cancer. Cancer, cancer. But I saw him here, right here. Do you want me to tell you where I saw him?"

14

Evils draw men together.
—Aristotle

ERNIE CARVER WAS staying incognito in the old Anderson cabin on the east side of Chelsea Pond. So said Larry Sedgwick. Larry Sedgwick said he saw Ernie. Larry said he saw a lot of things. Maybe it was true, maybe it wasn't. If it was, what brought Ernie to town? Benj was already in the ground; all that was taken care of. So Ernie was here to finish up some other affairs, maybe claim what Benj left. Why be so elusive? Well, Ernie was a Carver, and if Benj was eccentric, so was Ernie. Why not stay at Benj's place, unless Ernie was scared of ghosts? And what about the cancer in Arizona? Ernie Carver was supposed to be dying of cancer. He wouldn't travel back to Lyme to hide out in a weeded-over, abandoned cabin if he was dying of cancer, not unless something else was involved. It was all speculation, because Larry Sedgwick was the one who said he saw Ernie.

"Sarah," Hugh said into the telephone, "I've got a question."

"Now, Hugh, dear," said the demure, self-deprecating, omniscient voice, "I just work in this little office, but I'll help if I can. Did you find out anything about that Bill Kanin? He was such a pleasant young man. He reminded me of you when you were young."

"But not anymore, is that what you're saying, Sarah?"

"Of course, now, too," she said, her little-old-lady teasing tone coming through the wire. "Now, you know that I don't care too much for that Henry Perley that hired him, you know that."

"I know that."

"There's something about the way of his that just vexes me."

"I can understand that, Sarah. Now, about that question I had."

"Veda just the other day told me, in fact, that she heard something she just didn't like. She works over at the Perley place, you know, once a week. She cleans up and that sort of thing for Mrs. Perley. Now, Mrs. Perley is a nice woman, I have to say that. And she likes a clean house. That's what Veda told me. Anyway, she was telling me the other day that the last time she was over there in the kitchen mopping the floor, well, she heard Mr. Perley there in the front room and he was talking with two other men and when Mrs. Perley went to town Veda heard them say something about subdivisions and that sort of thing. Well, Veda didn't let on to Mrs. Perley, but she kind of found out who these men were just the same."

Hugh was pressing the receiver to his ear hard. "Who were they, Sarah?"

"Well, Veda said they were two men named Mr. Fratacelli and a Mr. Unger. Do you know them?"

"*Of* them, I do."

"Well, of course, they can talk all they want about subdivisions," Sarah said in her little, sweet, iron-bar voice, "but we have our ways in this office to see to it. You know that, Hugh, don't you?"

"That I know, Sarah. And these men knew Veda was there in the kitchen?"

"They ought to. She was there making noise mopping and things like that. It was only a door away. Anyway, I

118

thought that was interesting, what with all that business going on up there. Don't you think, Hugh, dear?"

"I do, Sarah."

"Now what exactly did you want?"

"Ah, yes. I was wondering if you heard about Ernie Carver. Someone said he was back in town. Have you seen him or heard that he was here?"

"Ernie? Oh, poor Ernie. No, I haven't. He has cancer, and I heard that he was in Arizona. He's supposed to be here in Lyme?"

"Well, maybe somebody must be mistaken."

"Somebody saw him up at Benj's place?"

"No, staying out at the old Anderson cabin."

"Why would he do that?"

"I don't know, Sarah. I'm not even sure that he's there."

"Well, why don't you find out, Hugh, dear? It's very simple, you know."

"How's that, Sarah?"

"Just go out to the Anderson cabin and see for yourself."

Being administered common sense by Sarah Baylord was one of the humiliating pills required of dealing with her. One had to suffer not merely the sudden sunshine thought of what she said but the baby-like brutality of her tone. Of *course,* if Hugh wanted to find out if Ernie Carver was staying at the old Anderson cabin, Hugh ought to go out there and see for himself. Of course. One did not need to steep one's mind in Plato's *Republic* to figure that out. One ought to be able to figure it out for oneself.

So Hugh, dear, before hanging up the phone, agreed with Sarah and said that was a good idea, he'd do that, why didn't he think of it in the first place. It was an opening that fearless Sarah entered: She told Hugh that *she* knew why he didn't think of that in the first place. Sarah Baylord had such an air of wolf-in-grandmother-clothes about her. She left the spicy thought dangling in New England Telephone Company wires while the two of them bade their good-byes.

Hugh stared at the quiet black phone on the receiver and tried to recover the momentum of his advanced education. He smiled and shook his head. Why did he feel so third-grade-ish? Because he was dealing with Sarah Baylord, that's why. The dagger darling.

He dialed Proctor Hammond.

"Speak."

"Quint."

"Oh."

"What do you know about Thomas Fratacelli? Ever heard of him?"

"I told you what I know—his license plate."

"Well, what do you know about Fratacelli and Arthur Unger and Henry Perley?"

"You don't want to know something. You want to tell me something."

"I'm drowning in common sense today."

"Common sense is what happens to common people."

"*Et tu, Brute.*"

"What you have to understand, Quint, is that you have the pieces but not the puzzle. Nothing too difficult about that. The problem is to think in gestalts. You know, stretch. Stretch. No killings without killers. So tell me what you want to tell me."

"I don't know what I want to tell you."

"You called to tell me that!"

"I called because I got three killings and it looks like we got some big-stakes land pressure brewing here. I'm hearing talk about subdivisions and lakeside condominiums and marinas. It's closing in. But it's too neat, too obvious, like train tracks. Something's not right."

120

"Three killings don't mean three killers."

"It doesn't mean *any* number of killers."

"*Et tu, Aristotle.* So you're telling me that million-dollar bulldozing is the motivation."

"It's moving that way."

"Now you need the opportunities."

"We're in the deep, dark woods, Proctor. The opportunities are around every maple tree. People are getting jumpy, nervous. They don't like it."

"Let's put it this way. Some loony with blood on his brain sees people in the way of million-dollar opportunities. Loony gets rid of people. Loony gets million-dollar opportunity."

"Here's the way it is. The Reed property is prime lakefront land. The Carver place is behind it; Benj Carver got killed. The Perley place behind Carver is owned by a big contractor who has big developers for tea and sympathy in his living room. All right, but then a surveyor that Perley hires is killed. I don't get it. He was killed on Benj Carver's property. Why is Perley going to kill the surveyor he hired?"

"You're saying Perley killed the surveyor."

"Maybe."

"You can't. You've got the pieces, but like I say, you don't have the puzzle until you keep turning the pieces inside and out and upside down."

"Maybe Perley doesn't care one way or another," Hugh said. "Maybe he has nothing to do with any of this."

"Maybe Western Civilization would have been different if Paul of Tarsus had had his way and the basis for the Christian church was Greek instead of Roman. Maybe if Holy Christ's big message, his only real message—'By ye fruits ye shall know them'—*kept* being the big message we'd have a different civilization, a better civilization, a *great* civilization. Maybe if Holy Christ's churches kept being churches instead of one big mammoth church, we'd be *holy* Christians. Maybe if Greek culture pervaded the church instead of Roman culture, we'd be a freer civilization, a just civilization, a *cultured* civilization, for God's sakes. Maybe . . ."

"All right, Proctor . . ."

". . . maybe if Christ's plan, which was to have all sorts of little churches spread around the empire, which was what he believed because he hated dogma, that's what he was fighting against in the first place, he *hated* the establishment, what it was doing, what do you think he was up against, maybe if the Greek idea took root instead of the Roman we'd have some respect for art in this civilization, this so-called culture of ours, we'd have some tolerance and humanity, some respect for *ideas,* for Christ's sakes, some respect for intellect and reasoning powers, some respect for freedom, individual *freedom.* That was the Greek gift and we threw it away. If we had real respect for freedom, then maybe misfits like you, Hugh Quint . . ."

"Oh, yes, Proctor Hammond . . ."

". . . wouldn't be misfits but just ordinary human individuals, free-spirited, Greek-loving, Greek-*glory* individuals who didn't have to fight the whole damn world because you might have some sort of teeny-weeny maverick idea and you don't work in an insurance company living off the life savings of goddamn *widows.* Maybe we'd have a saner world, a rational world, we wouldn't be fighting all that occult escapism black magic murdering mysticism that lives on fear and power instead of reason and intellect. Everybody wouldn't be so quick to abandon the one great gift we've got—our *brains*— because they'd be living by their brains instead of their barbarism . . ."

"I got it, Proctor . . ."

". . . But no, no, all the quivering little churches

around the empire had to look to the Rome church, the church of Rome, next to the emperor for protection, and what'd we get? We got a civilization of laws and dogma and big, smothering authority that crushed out that Greek freedom. We got form instead of action. Mouth the right words and you're safe, brother, safe. No torture on the rack this week. No thumb screws this month. So the church of *Rome,* not the churches of Christ and Greece, put the screws to Western civilization and we got what we've got."

"I got it, Proctor."

"You can do your maybes all you want, Quint. But maybes aren't what *is.* So, *maybe* what's his name . . ."

"Perley."

"So maybe Perley had nothing to do with all this and maybe he doesn't care, but maybe doesn't change history, and what is *is.*"

"You're in hot form today, Proctor."

"I'm always in hot form."

"So philosophical."

"Philosophy is what should be."

"Ought to be."

"I deal in what is."

"I never saw a science that built a civilization."

"That's supposed to be something profound, I take it."

"Only as profound as such a thought can last without changing. Let's face it, Proctor. Ptolemy's science of astronomy isn't your example of scientific longevity."

"It worked for the time."

"But it didn't build the time."

"No one thing builds an era."

"Rule by the people instead of a potentate did."

"It was practical."

"It was just. People governed should have a say in how they're governed, just as people who labor to make wealth should have a share in the wealth they make."

"This has some relevance to this Perley character, I take it. You're driving up to a grand conclusion. You're taking advantage of my exposition of Western civilization."

"I would never do such a vicious thing."

"Don't ignore this Perley. Don't maybe him out of the picture. Don't maybe anybody out."

"A new element's in the picture, too."

"Check it out."

"I'm going to. Right now."

"It's the grain of sand that makes the pearl."

"Never heard of that before."

"Smart philosophical ass. And *you* called *me*."

The same road that went to Amos's place went to the old Anderson cabin, farther along. It wound through the birches and hemlocks, maples and beech, getting bumpier, more rutted. In full summer, weeds would be growing tall in the high ground between the wheel grooves.

The road was set back enough from the shore to hide it from the water and curved around the dogleg of the east side of the pond. Hugh stopped at the boulder that winter erosion had toppled in the way. His were the only car tracks.

Twilight was still bright enough to see Amos's place through the woods, barely; the light was going fast. The other way he couldn't see the Anderson cabin, but it was only a little way, if he remembered right.

If Larry was right, dinner time was good to catch Ernie there. But who knew about Larry Sedgwick? He could be watching Hugh right now from some boulder or behind an oak, out roaming to do his watching, maybe seeing something, maybe not, maybe seeing something that wasn't there.

The terrain turned into a steep incline toward the pond

as the outcrops and overhangs of Webster's Rocks, an overlooking mountain, rose up.

Then came the thin-sliced confusion of what struck him first—the sense of presence or the click of footsteps, the mind working its wonders. He stopped short and listened. Someone watching him was in the woods, he felt it, the way the dark suddenly crowded him. When his feet stopped, so in the undefined distance did the others, but only after the telltale milliseconds, not quite overlapping, not quite matching.

He fought the panic of the dark, the spectre of those rifle shots through the windows, of Davy Tefler strangled tight to the tree.

Heart pounding hard.

The quiet anticipated the menacing echo of the shot; the shot never came.

He heard nothing.

It was a waiting game. Then the fast-cracking twigs, the scamper on rock and mud, loose pebbles. To the right. Above him.

15

The best laid schemes o' mice an' men.
—Robert Burns

HUGH STUDIED THE blackness overhead, the moonless, actionless wall of midnight. The disembodied noises. Starlight slivered the trees and the rocky overhang. He couldn't see much. The running sound headed toward the north side of the pond, along the protruding mid-side of the cliff. He knew the trail up there. It connected with the trail below and then angled left up the cliff.

Who the hell was it?

Instinct—gut curiosity—thrust him forward. He ran through the brush for the bottom trail, the one along the jumbled edge of the pond.

He heard the roll of pebbles down the cliff ahead. The sneak knew the territory but was kicking notices along the way. Heading for the trail junction.

The bottom trail was for tourists, easy when the boulders were in the sun. But run too fast and you fall. Run slow. Watch the logs. Watch the pits.

The wind lay dead in its tracks; the pond looked walkable. The water was immense as it spread murky in the snuffed starlight. Hugh caught its edge out his eye as he twisted in and out the tumble of granite blocks, mammoth, cold, mindless obstacles. You couldn't maneuver around this part of the pond without a trail, not Hugh, not the sneak. Sniper? No, Hugh would have been already shot dead, or missed.

The pebbles kept clinking down the cliff ahead. The runner was making better time than Hugh. Where the hell was that junction? Too many boulders for a trail. In and out. Too easy to crack an ankle. Fall and your skull's split.

The thudding explosion of granite rock against granite tucked Hugh to his knees. It could have been granite against his head, split and smashed.

This was absurd. What was Hugh doing chasing the son-of-a-bitch through these body-mangling shadows? A hand-size rock thrown at that height could spill his brains. He was asking for the morgue.

Ah, but panic was on the run up the cliff, not Hugh. The son-of-a-bitch was the one kicking signals of where he was. That told something.

Then a fresh slip of pebbles and rocks overhead, somewhere in the pitch.

There was only the sound. Then the pinging and thudding stopped, and the dull sound of boot on boulder replaced it. The runner had reached the trail, home clear, on up the cliff to the top.

Hugh moved on, resisting the urge to cut across the rough, slanted terrain, to shortcut the connecting trail.

The goddamn puny sign at the junction was worthless. Who could see that at night? He would've missed it except for the maverick glint off the chiseled yellow letters. Goddamn puny arrow pointing to Webster's Rocks, left and up.

The Rocks flattened out some at the top. If you were seventeen, you took your sixteen-year-old girlfriend up there (or, sly maneuvering, she took you up there), and you made sure it was night. Lyme didn't have too many pairs, so it was a good chance that you'd be alone and have the whole mountain to yourself. You brought some beer and cigarettes, and matches because you thought ahead a lot about Webster's Rocks. You said to her,

"Let's go up to Webster's," but to the other guys, you said, "I took her up to the Rocks," and they said, "You get off them all right?" That, of course, was the vaudevillian tag line as you danced off the glory scene, curtain down, grins and slugs on the biceps. If you took some rot-gut, mouth-wretched whiskey and, lucky import from the netherworld, some grass, you were hot shit. You giggled and got loose, and because you were two years away from the apex of virility and too potent for failure, you never learned what Shakespeare said: "Drink provokes the desire but takes away the performance."

You went up there in conglomerates, too, but always in equal assigned pairs of male and female, laughing and joking and figuring that *this* was the time for one of those Roman orgies you read about in Ancient History. Summer nights with plenty of moonlight. Beer parties in the caves up there. You learned about it from older brothers and sisters when you were in the sixth grade—wicked stuff, but when you grew up you knew you'd end up in those caves, too. Can I go? you asked. When you're older, they said, and if you tell Mom I'll *get* you.

The caves were for fires at the entrances, for standing around with beer cans in your hands, the girls laughing and teasing. You burned frankfurters black as crayons and ate them anyway. Somebody always said, "We got the hot dogs, you girls bring the buns?" Never failed. Sex giggles and guffaws. The scared ones stayed by the fire, but the others took a half-flaming log and led the scary exploration with Stone Age torch in hand into the Lethe reaches of the inner crevices of the caves. Jittery shadows followed you and there, lurking in the alimentary canal of the earth, ready to acidify you into planetary stomach debris, were the monster fears of the species, only you didn't know it yet in precisely that way. You didn't get far because the torch was burning down (How did the Stone Agers do it?) and the girls, practical even at that age, led you back.

Rumors told you that the caves could swallow you to China, if you made one false move. When you got back, only one couple remained at the fire, to watch it. Your parents trained you well, although you would have denied it with passion. They told you that the others went off to other caves or someplace in the dark and who knew what they were doing? Grins. Maybe what you were doing in that cave. The last couple that returned looked positively, totally ransacked; their shirts were smudged with dust and dirt, their hair full of pine needles, their mouths smeared and worn. So someone had to say to cock robin, "Did you go into the cave?" and cock robin said, "Wouldn't you like to know?" The girls giggled glances at each other as the boys burst out loud at this hilarious retort and shoved each other off balance.

Now the ancient rumors of the caves crowded Hugh's head. Anybody could get lost in them; they twisted and turned, dead-ended, dropped into bottomless pits. Hugh's quarry was going for them.

Hugh knew the caves, but he hadn't seen them in years. They were up there in the night. They *were* the night. He pictured them as he remembered them: craggy, convoluted façades with quick darknesses a few feet inside. They were like skyscrapers, one after another, freaks in the rolling woodlands. They stirred curiosity because they were so out of place.

He climbed to them, his breath labored more in effort now than exhilaration. The caves could lose people; that was their reputation, but the son-of-a-bitch wasn't running to lose. Maybe it was a diversion. Maybe he knew that Hugh knew the caves, figured that Hugh figured the man would hide in the crawly corners, never found, only that he might have headed out beyond the caves, below them, around them. Who knows?

As Hugh climbed, the sound of muffled boots stopped. He stopped, too, and listened; he heard his breath. He moved on, slower. Up the trail. It was leveling out. You walked flat, sort of, to reach the caves; he remembered that. He kept to the edge of the trail, moved fast from trunk to trunk. The pines were thinning. He stopped and listened hard. Nothing.

He waited, and nothing.

The voiceless caves were up ahead, rippled and blocky in the night, Egyptianlike, if Mother Earth were Father Pharaoh.

What the hell was Hugh doing? Let the bastard go. He wasn't panicking. He was too calculating, suckering Hugh.

Hugh crouched at a chunky mushroom of a boulder and studied the pillared caves. Maybe the bastard was long gone. Why not? The only eyes on him were owl eyes. But check it out, Quint; once trained, always trained. Besides, the son-of-a-bitch sneak thief almost crowned him with that goddamn rock.

He slid along the granite, weaving in and out of the protrusions and bulges like a fat shadow, hands on rock, eyes on caves. He had made it this far without getting shot at, so that eliminated that possibility—no rifle. Maybe it *was* crazy Larry, and Hugh was scaring the hell out of him. So don't think killer slug burning your heart out; think of wringing a trap. Whoever the rock-thrower was was in those caves.

He crept toward the first ripple of caves, racing and ducking from shelter to shelter, protection to protection. He edged to a thick pine growing bent from an unsympathetic boulder. A full minute later, he crouched and scampered over the exposed corrugated terrain to the side of the first row of caves.

He climbed the side, fleshy hands gripping bloodless rock, skinning his fingers. Then he crept over the top, crouching away from the sheer assailability of his back, tiptoeing almost like in slippers, which was ridiculous, he knew it, because this was no fiberglass dome with killers inside ready to blast the roof off and Hugh Quint besides.

He settled down high on the brow of the caves, looking down. And waited.

A half hour.

Nothing. Who could stay in those caves alone like that?

He gave it another half hour, and then he felt the scheme empty itself. All he wanted was maybe crown the son-of-a-bitch with a chunk of granite, like he almost got. It wasn't going to happen.

The bastard was as patient as he was. He was going to have to go in and see, smoke him out with something. Yeah, with fire.

No matches.

He crept down the front of the wrinkled cliff and picked the second cave, the one with the gaping, ghoulish, toothless mouth to the depths. He studied the stillness, the sullen, angular, taut invitation to enter this sleeping rockface. Go ahead, wake it. See if the jaws snap. Those damn bad spectres again.

He moved to the side of the big black mouth, running as fast as the mountain let him, crouching again in the strung silence to see if his unnerving shadows unnerved the other shadows. They didn't.

No ruminating sounds burped up the dark gullet, no kicked pebbles or scraped boots. He waited.

He remembered those nasty warehouse hunts. The dank, foggy Boston waterfront warehouse hunts. He and his partner ran down this slavering punk into a cobwebby monster of a building. Rats knew their territory, and this rat knew that building. He and his partner split right inside the same crevice the punk disappeared into, and then they froze, lead drawn, listening. Nothing. The punk was there all right, trying to smother his panting, freezing into one of the black corners, salting away like Lot's wife.

Then Hugh and his partner stepped in an opposite circumference to close in on the rat, strangle the punk with their creeping presence. He couldn't escape without noise. The place was a junk heap—planks to trip over, plaster to crunch, beer cans to kick, a mess. One step and their ears would cock to the guy's first move.

So Hugh and his partner waited. Stood still. Letting the rat tick his panic into gear. Ten minutes, fifteen minutes of extraterrestrial silence. Rats couldn't sit still.

This one did. They lost him, slipped out a hole in the wall maybe, but which hole? What did it matter? He was gone.

Hugh studied the caves again, this time more with his ears. When he slinked inside, no matter what, his silhouette was going to show. Mountains didn't move, he did. From the inside, he was going to be plastered gray against the muted backdrop of the cave entrance. He didn't have his cave eyes yet. Maybe he should stir some panic; throw in a rock. Stay out. Stay alive.

He picked up a pebble, hesitated, and finger-snapped it inside, diagonally. It hit somewhere opposite him in the pitch dark, a tantalizing tingle of noise like, he hoped, someone creeping inside to strangle the son-of-a-bitch panicked rat.

Nothing.

He waited, and then he eased like a liquid shadow farther into the liquid pitch, or so he thought.

The son-of-a-bitch sniper-shot blasted the cave with a TNT sound, jerking Hugh spastically against the stabbing granite chunks, his heart flooding his gut. A tremendous thundering, echoing blast.

The flare of the rifle flashed the cave into an orangy glaze of giant teethlike shadows ready to chomp him.

132

The explosion tightened his head away from it, and all he could see was the reflection, not the source. It was somewhere back there.

He waited for the pain of death, a horrible bleeding wound. It didn't come.

He heard the scrape of boots, sliding, thumping, running, more scraping. The cave puréed it together. The universal light turned to universal blackness. Sound without direction: echoes that drenched every part of Hugh except the bottom of his feet.

He waited for the second shot.

He was a sitting duck. He could have been plugged between the eyes.

He edged deeper into the cave gullet, toward the sounds of the retreating rat and the rifle clanking against granite with only the faintest of direction. Killer climbing out the escape hole. Up? Down? Who could tell?

The shot was to frighten. He was too easy not to kill.

Then the rat noise stopped. Not suddenly, just muffled away. That was the puzzle.

Hugh froze and listened. He almost got his brains drained down there on the mountain, climbed the goddamn mountain, waited, got suckered in, got shot at. Helpless moth at the killer flame, mesmerized. The mind said no, Stone Age instinct said move on, body, you're hooked. Get some more, flush out the rat. Rats can't fly.

He crouched farther in, pressing against the protruding drippy walls, erasing his silhouette, feeling inches ahead with hands and feet. He'd force the bastard into a dead-end trap. Then what? Get killed? Big dead hero. Get out of there, and fast.

A quick glance back showed what a stupid gunless target he was, framed by the entrance like he figured, starlight the killer accomplice. Get out of there!

He heard the noise as he looked back. Outside the cave. The sniper was on his way down the cliff.

Out the rat hole.

Out another cave.

All that trapping noise that muffled away was just the sniper disappearing down some drainpipe in the system to the basement door.

Hugh stumbled his way back to the mouth-face of the cave. In the now vast blackened gorge of the world below, he heard the distant, unshielded, unsecret scamper of a triumphant rat making his way down the mountainside, surefooted and home free, with a rifle that wasn't supposed to be in his hands.

16

Human Kind cannot bear very much reality.
　　　　　　　　　—T. S. Eliot

HUGH MADE IT straight away to Janice at her beacon cabin in the woods, drawn to her for rebirth, a moth attracted to a different kind of flame. He was shot at and suckered out of his wits on the mountain. Who needed that, and who needed to think about it?

She opened the door to his knock, and there she was with her magnetizing smile. Already he felt better, wanted, triumphant, and he hadn't even stepped inside.

In he went with more impulse than he could account for as base reaction to being buffeted by the cruel world. Seeing her was more like its own separate impulse.

"What've you been *doing?*" she asked, taking in his smudged shirt and the smear mark of dirt or mud or something on the thigh side of his pants.

"Getting shot at," he said. At first it was a simple truth, but it turned fast into a truth with a thrashing need for comfort and joy.

She led him to the center of the room where the light cast him clear and full, held her hands on each of his arms, and studied him. "Hugh," she said, "what happened?"

He told her: He got shot at. All he wanted to do was find out who was staying at the old Anderson place; he heard that Ernie Carver was in town. Larry told him, but who could be sure of Larry? So he went out there. And got shot at (Did she hear that? Was she worried at all?) and tracked the sniper down. He didn't even have a gun. (Pretty brave, huh? Does she really have to know how many times he was shot at?) So he followed him up the trail to Webster's Rocks. He could hardly see, it was so dark, but he could hear. And then the guy heaved a huge boulder that missed him by *inches.* Have you ever hunted somebody up there? At night? (Of course not. Only men do that.) What was he trying to prove? He had enough of that stuff in Boston, but, hell, getting shot at *enrages* you. You got to do something about it or you feel, well, you feel enraged. So he heard this sound in the caves. She knew the caves up there. He followed the sound inside. (Scary, right?) No, first he climbed on top of the caves and he waited there. Just waited, how long he didn't know. Hours, probably. He couldn't tell. He was going to clobber that sniper when he moved out of there. But that sniper, and he meant a *sniper,* like in some guerilla war someplace, stayed put. (She's getting the picture—this is tough stuff.) He didn't know who it was, but it was somebody who knew the scene. Anyway, he waited there, looking down on the caves. It was hard to see, it was *dark,* but not as dark as in the caves. Anyway, he just stayed put because sooner or later that rifle (Well, she didn't exactly have to know that he really didn't know about a rifle at that particular point) was going to poke out someplace to see what was happening. But nothing happened. *Nothing* happened. He thought he blew it. That damn sniper wasn't in those caves at all. Then he crawled down the front and decided he'd check it out. He'd go *into* one of those caves and see for himself. (Did she hear that?) So he went in. Goddamn, another *shot!* Scared the hell out of him. He thought the whole cave was going to blow up, and he couldn't see anything. Big flash and this huge explosion. Scared the hell out of him. What could he do? He had to do

136

something. (A man had to do something.) He was a sitting duck. But the shot hit someplace, he didn't know where. He banged himself against the wall. Probably had bruises all over. Then he heard this sound in the back of the cave. Yes, she was right, he should have gotten out of there (Ah, she cares), but when you're shot at you just get *enraged* or something. He didn't know what, but he thought he could pin the sucker back into a corner someplace. Yes, he knew he didn't have a gun, it was in someone else's hands, but something got to him and he just kept going at it. So he heard this sound and then it stopped. He thought the cave was a trap, a dead end or something, or maybe a big pit. (You see how dangerous it was?) Then this sound stopped. He turned around and he heard this other sound outside. He went out there and heard this goddamn killer sniper running down the mountain. Yeah, he knew he almost got killed. Yes, yes, he should have let go, but when a man gets into a situation like that you have to do something (A man has to do something, right?). All he wanted to do was see who it was, and deal with it later. He knew he almost got shot. He wouldn't do it again. He promised. He really did.

"You better."

"Now let's talk about you."

"Well, it wasn't too exciting today at work. I didn't get shot at."

"Not even once?"

"Someone tried to throw a misplaced modifier at me, but that's about it."

"You ducked."

"I did."

"Did you twist your back?"

"No, only my pencil."

"Oh, too bad."

"You want me to wrench my back, is that it?"

"No, I just thought you might like a back rub."

"Oh. Well, I might."

He smiled and stretched his open hand to the back of her neck and slid his fingers back and forth.

"Hhmmm," she sighed, twisting her head. "Come to think of it, I did sort of strain my back."

"It needs some rubbing, maybe."

"I think so."

"A little massage does wonders."

"It does."

"I can imagine."

"I can, too."

"We both can."

"We can," she said, smiling.

He reached both arms behind her, slid his hands under her blue-flowered kick-around shirt, and drew the palms of his hands flat up and down against her back.

"Uummm."

"I was hoping that might feel good, wrenched backs being what they are."

"They *are* troublesome."

"I see you've removed your bra."

"You never know who might drop in."

"True."

"Uummm."

"There's something invigorating about a back rub, isn't there?"

"There is."

"I can feel it all over."

"I can, too."

"It's kind of vertical here though, isn't it?"

"It is. Uummm."

"Is it all vertical in this place?"

"No."

"It isn't?"

"Uummm."

"Where do you think it isn't?"
"I know just the place."
"You do?"
"Uh huh."
"Where?"
"Back there."
"Where's that?"
"Uummm."
"Where?"
"Back there."
"In that room back there?"
"Uh huh."
"Back there?"
"Uh huh."

The next glorious, cleansed, realigned morning, reinvigorated Hugh Quint continued where he left off—the old Anderson cottage. If watchful Larry was loonisizing again, maybe the on-and-off again goblin really did see Ernie Carver. Hugh couldn't tell for sure by the outside of the cabin. Weeds were waist high, but then somebody had been there because a channel of tall grass was bent to the door.

"Hello? Anybody here?"

When nobody answered, Hugh stepped to the unpainted plank-wood door and knocked. "Anybody here?"

He waited and listened for some stirring inside. Then as he leaned to peer in the window, he jerked to a stop.

"Depends."

The voice had a hint of watch-your-step.

Hugh turned to see a thin, steady-eyed man at a maple tree to the right. "Ah, there is," he said in reflex, defensive at the intrusion. The man had his mouth smiling more than the word and his voice. He was not meant just to be heard; his folded face had a relaxed tone to it, although he was having fun misleading Hugh with a Western false-front facade, Eastern style.

"Saw you coming. Do I know you?"

"No, I don't think so. Hugh Quint."

The old man made no sign of recognition or interest. He might as well have been sledgehammering a concrete wall and kept on doing it. He didn't offer his name, and maybe he wouldn't. Depended.

"I wasn't sure anyone was staying here," Hugh said, smiling, ingratiating.

"Abandoned."

"It's an old-timer," Hugh said, and then embellished that with an affectionate smile as he waved appreciation for the cottage, with its proper shutters and sturdy woodsiness, its no-nonsense, four-square corners, two front windows, one door, one brick chimney. Its aloneness, its omnipotent patience.

The man had the Carver mouth all right, as if drawn across a pug face with a number two pencil. His blue eyes of old age had circled back to watery baby innocence. His frame sagged more than drooped under the husky red plaid shirt, which maybe confirmed the rumor that Benj's brother had cancer and moved out to Arizona. He was thinner than Carver stock; it looked like sick thinness, the kind that chocolate eclairs didn't remedy, the kind no one mentioned too much.

"Anderson place," the old man said. "You know him?"

"No. That was before my time."

"Thought so. He told me once, 'Ernie,'—you know who I am."

Hugh nodded.

"He said, 'Ernie, anytime you need a place to stay, you stay here.' So here I am."

"I'm sorry about Benj."

Ernie Carver made no reaction. On he went. "So when I don't want to stay at Benj's place, I stay here. Too crowded up at his place. There's that Amos guy right next door, you know what I mean?"

Hugh made a figure eight of his head—yes and no, getting it all in: Watch whom you're agreeing with, you never know.

"So I stay out here."

"And then people like me come out looking for you."

"Didn't figure anybody knew I was here, tell the truth."

Hugh shrugged. "It's a small town. So how long you staying, Ernie?"

Ernie grinned, showing he knew what Hugh wanted to know: Why was he here. You didn't ask too much on a direct line to old-timers like Ernie Carver. You got to know what they wanted you to know, one way or another. The rest was guesswork.

"Been in Arizona, you know."

Hugh nodded enough to show he knew the cancer rumors, enough to show some sympathy. Maybe Ernie was back here for one last visit, that sort of thing.

"Have to look to a few things at Benj's, you know. But I figure to stay out here away from all that town stuff, people cornering you at the post office. You got to pick and choose, you know."

Like Amos, Hugh thought, but never in a thousand years would he say it aloud. The more Ernie talked, the more Amos appeared. The same blood coursed the veins, it was just that Type Amos didn't mix with Type Ernie.

"You got to pick and choose," Ernie repeated, waiting.

Hugh picked up the clue and said, "I know what you mean. It can get crowded even when you see one or two people a day. I get that way myself sometimes. You see somebody you know on the desert someplace and pretty soon it's a whole mob."

Ernie grinned and nodded.

"Then you're in New York City in the middle of lunch hour and you're alone."

Ernie said, "Yep."

"Well," Hugh said, stuffing his hands into his pockets, "guess I should be going. Don't want to crowd you."

Ernie grinned and said, "Nope, don't do that."

"I won't tell anybody you're here."

"You got to pick and choose. Benj and Amos picked and choosed, didn't they? Only they picked and choosed against each other, and can't blame them neither, what the Reeds did to the Carvers. You know about that."

Hugh nodded and shrugged.

"You been here long enough for that. Now Benj, I told him he should come out to Arizona and see me, and he says to me, 'I ain't going out there to die.' Well, what can you do with somebody like that?"

"You can't figure."

"You can't figure," Ernie echoed, eyes steady on as usual, and maybe he was telling about his cancer but he wasn't one to make it unmistakable.

"You need anything?"

Ernie shook his head good and slow, lips pursed. What a question *that* was.

"Well, Ernie, I'll see you."

"No, you can't figure," said Ernie Carver, not ready to release Hugh. Age had its grip. "I'm the only real Carver left and I'm going over the edge pretty soon, and so you got to see to some things you left behind. That's the way it is when you're my age, my condition. You know about it."

Hugh spread his hands in recognition. At first he thought the old man didn't know who he was. He was changing his mind. He heard something.

"So I came back to see to Benj and all that. Do right by him."

"You have to."

"I figure."

They fell silent, looked away, Ernie left, Hugh right.

Ernie scratched his beard stubble, drawing his spread forefinger and thumb down his cheeks and jaw bones to the chin point. "Yep. Kind of hard to figure things, the way life goes. The things you do for strangers."

"It's hard to figure."

"Yep."

Hugh waited for the old man to say what he wanted to say, what he wanted Hugh to know. It was coming plain, the gap was just about open enough, and it wasn't what Hugh expected. The words threw him off kilter.

"You know," Ernie said, "that Perley guy's the one that got me back here. Said he had to talk to me. Paid my ticket, flew me back. You just can't figure."

17

Fury ministers arms.
—Virgil

HUGH WAS FLABBERGASTED that Henry Perley would brash his way into the Reed and Carver feud, but there it was. Perley had sought out Ernie in Arizona, flown him back, and was scheming how to get Ernie to sell Benj's land when the inheritance was settled, the title transferred, and the time was right. He was playing Carver line against Reed line.

In a rush, Hugh headed straight for Amos and found him outside hammering the sagging woodshed back in place after the long haul of winter snow on it. He looked up once.

"Got an idea," Hugh said, "and I want to see what you think of it."

"Sure you do." Amos went on hammering.

"Have I got your attention?"

"You NEED it?" Amos shouted.

"That's the idea, Amos."

Amos stopped hammering. "THAT'S your idea? That's what you want to tell me?"

"No, of course not."

"You want to come here, interrupt my fixing, and tell me your idea is to get my attention?"

"Amos, come on."

"Come on where?"

Hugh grinned and shook his head. "You're giving me a hard time."

"You think I got nothing to do but give you a hard time?" he shouted. "I *work* around here, you know. Shed isn't fixing itself, you know. You got to WORK around here."

"I know that, Amos, but I was thinking about Benj's land and all that."

"WHAT ABOUT IT?"

"Well, nothing exactly, but . . ."

"That's your idea?"

"No, I'm trying to tell you."

"NOTHING EXACTLY?"

"I'm trying to tell you, Amos."

"You said that."

"I know, Amos, if you give me a chance, I'll tell you about it. Give me a chance."

"I'm giving you a chance. Go ahead. Here's your chance. Go on, go on, tell me your idea." Then he went back to slamming the hammer against the woodshed, head bent, ornery and cussed.

"I was thinking . . ."

"YEAH." Hammer, hammer.

". . . about what we could do to flush out all this business about Benj and that surveyor, Davy Tefler . . ."

"YEAH." Hammer, hammer.

"I was thinking of setting some bait and see what happens. What's going on here is that somebody's after the land around here . . ."

"YEAH." Hammer, hammer.

". . . So if we got somebody to say that they were going to sell their land, then whoever's behind this would think they got the scare tactics working, the pressure's on and it's working. It might bring somebody out in the open, force his hand. You know what I mean?"

"YEAH." Hammer, hammer.

"So I'm wondering, Amos, what you think? What do you think?"

"ABOUT WHAT?" Hammer, hammer.

"About putting out the word that you're thinking of selling your land."

"WHAT!" He stopped hammering; he bolted upright, his eyes flaring red. His neck tightened like it was going to squeeze off his head. "WHAT?"

Hugh sort of leaned backward, hands spread.

"You want me to sell MY LAND?"

Hugh twisted his hands so that they held him up for surrender. "I didn't say that, Amos. I don't want you to sell your land. I just thought you could *say* you were thinking about it. You're not actually going to do it."

"I AIN'T SELLING MY LAND."

"I know, Amos. I don't want you to. I didn't say that. But we got people killed around here. Benj. Right next to you. Somebody's forcing you out."

"NOBODY'S FORCING ME OUT."

"I know that, Amos, but they think they're doing it. Let's let them think it. Make them think that."

"Who's THEM?"

"I don't know. That's what I'm trying to find out. It's time to force their hand, get them out in the open."

"You keep saying THEM." He took his hammer and whacked it against the shed with two mightly blows. The shed shivered under the impact.

"Just say you're going to sell your land. You're just thinking about it," Hugh said, seeing the blood vessels in Amos's red neck elevated purple.

"When I say something, I MEAN it," Amos shouted. He glanced over his shoulder in defiance, the cobra look of venom making sure that Hugh Quint saw that he was astounded that anybody could think otherwise.

"I know that, Amos."

"You're telling me you don't."

Hugh surrendered again. "All right," he said, patting the air in front of him, "I'm just trying to think of something."

146

"Think of something else. I ain't going to sell MY LAND."

"I don't want you to, Amos."

"Heard different." He went back to hammering, and they both listened to the whacks on poor wood, mighty smashes that rocked the shed with not a twinge of human mercy.

"It's just an idea," Hugh said at last.

"Wrong idea."

Hugh paused. "What about this? What if somebody else says you're thinking about selling your land? That way you don't say it, but the word is out."

"The IDEA is out." He whacked the shed. "Here's what you do. YOU say I'm thinking of selling my land and I say you're a horse-whippin', thievin', cheatin' LIAR. How's that?"

"That's not the point, Amos."

"Whose point?"

Hugh surrendered again. "All right, Amos, all right. I was just trying to get something going here before somebody else gets hurt. Maybe gets killed."

Amos straightened up and stared bloodless boulders at him. "You saying I'm getting killed?"

"I'm not saying that at all."

"Heard different."

"I wasn't referring to you."

"Who?"

"Nobody, Amos. Just in general."

"No general around here."

"Oh, yeah?"

Amos glowered his V-deep eyebrows at Hugh, thrust his Roman chin out. "Get another idea," he said, his ragged bassoon voice as unwavering as his clamped-tight mouth.

"OK, Amos."

"Now, you going to help me fix this shed?"

"There's something else."

"Always is, when there's work to do."

"You know Ernie Carver?"

"That toothless old sawhorse, yeah, I know him. He's out in Arizona, dying or something. Who knows, and who cares? He's a CARVER."

"He's in town."

"WHAT?"

Hugh nodded.

"Who told you?"

"Larry."

Amos sniffed disgust: How could Hugh Quint believe it.

"It turned out to be true, I saw him myself. He's staying out at the old Anderson place. He's here all right. I talked with him."

"You would, SURE YOU WOULD."

"He told me something you should know."

"What? The earth's flat?"

Hugh ignored it. "He said Henry Perley brought him out here. Flew him out. Bought his ticket, because Perley had something to discuss with him."

"What?"

"He didn't say. But guess on it, Amos."

Amos Reed studied Hugh Quint. Then he gripped the hammer like an ax and whacked the living shivers out of the shed. He turned upright to Hugh and shouted, "He's getting even with me, Benj, that old, broken-down mud BOOT. Right through his own Carver brother. That's what he's doing. He's going to sell that land to PERLEY and Perley's going to CHAINSAW IT DOWN. He's going to CHAINSAW IT DOWN."

Hugh was about to say, *It's his land.* He changed his mind.

Amos raised his hand with the hammer like the Statue of Liberty and brandished it like Fury on fire. What an

148

actor. Give him control lessons and he could have been the greatest Shakespearean trouper of the century. His eyes were sparking flint chips, his cheeks were tighter than horsehide. "ERNIE CARVER! He's a no-good, cheatin', lyin', horsetail in the wind, that flat-faced old geezer, he's got cramps in his BRAINS, he ain't *got* no brains. He's no more than a TOAD, he's a TOAD-BRAINED traitor. TRAITOR! Going to Arizona—ARIZONA!—to die, that honey-bucket dodo bird can't wipe his nose without somebody telling him HOW TO DO IT, that old wreck. The old soused two-bit traitor can't tell the difference between two and *three*."

He whacked the shed.

"Don't tell ME about Ernie CARVER, he'd steal your stone WALL if he could put his boots on the right foot. What an old pile of cow plop, the TRAITOR going out there and coming back *here* to plague me, that's what he's doing, he's PLAGUING me, and Benj made him do it."

He whacked the shed again. Hugh stepped back.

"You hear me? He's PLAGUING me. He steps on MY LAND and he's going to be this SHED." He clobbered that shed and it shook hard. "Go ahead, tell him. He's going to be this SHED." Whack. Whack. Whack.

The phone rang as Hugh ran through the door after it. He picked it up in mid-ring.

"There you are," Rita said. "I've been trying to get you all day."

"I've been out."

"I heard that Ernie Carver is back in town," she said, stopping her husky, rapid-fire voice, letting the thunder sound in the silence.

She'd probably been talking with Amos. Or Amos with her. "He is. Talked with him myself."

"That's what I heard," she said, the urgency loud and

clear. "You know what this means, don't you, Hugh? He's here to make deals with Benj's land, the Carver place, and that's the beginning of the end if anything gets going on it. I know how all this works, Hugh. That's what all these shootings are about, I'm telling you. Scare the locals and out come the Lone Ranger developers to save the day, only they're saving themselves, not us. I've seen it happen all over the place. First, you get the appetite for greed rolling, or you panic them. Then you come in with the savior news, buy up at a penny an acre, and then chainsaw it all down."

She was talking to Amos, all right. "It's not to that point, Rita."

"Not yet."

"Sounds like some panic in you," Hugh said nice and easy. "That doesn't help."

"It's not panic. It's the alarm. I'm sounding the alarm, and I've been doing it so long it gets me all upset. I just see it coming. Anybody can, if they just look a little. I've been looking a lot, and that's what scares me. Ernie's back here for no good reason. Now, I'm sorry about Benj and all that, but, let's face it, what's done is done and we got some watching to do on Ernie or he's going to start dealing with Perley real soon."

"In the last analysis," said Hugh, vagrant lawyer, "it's Carver land and the Carvers can do what they want with it."

"Try telling that to Amos."

"I tried."

"We could put the land in a conservancy."

"You think Ernie is going to do that? Especially if Amos doesn't? Either one would do the opposite of the other, anyway."

"I don't know," Rita said, sighing hard, letting Hugh know that her mouth was needle tight. "I don't know."

"I don't know either, Rita."

150

"Anyway, it worries me, it worries me a lot. Ernie's not as bad as his brother, but . . ."

"But he's a Carver."

"Right."

The spaghetti Hugh ate for dinner splattered on his shirt, but the shirt was sort of red in the first place. He made the sauce with a can of Italian plum tomatoes, sautéed the onions in butter and oil, added chopped garlic clove, oregano, chopped parsley, some tomato paste to thicken it, a little salt, a little pepper. What was difficult? Twenty minutes and fresh.

The phone rang when he was mopping the sauce with a chunk of Italian bread. "Been thinking," Amos said. No hello, no nothing.

"Amos."

"Been thinking about that Ernie Carver, that skunk traitor. You know who I mean. You seen him."

"I did."

"Been thinking about what I just did, and I'm feeling good about it."

"What'd you just do, Amos?"

"Went up to that Perley place and I told that Genghis Khan Hitler what I thought of him."

Hugh pressed his head to the receiver. "You what?"

"Going DEAF?"

"Amos, I'm coming up there."

"Then I told him what you said."

"What?"

"I told him I was selling my land."

"Amos, you should've let me handle this."

"And gum it all up?"

18

Half the truth is often a great lie.
—Benjamin Franklin

HUGH GRABBED A Hershey bar for dessert, slipped the nearest shirt-jacket on his back, and headed for Amos's place. Ovid said something about how more made him poor. Or was it Pliny? He bought one Hershey bar at a time. It made him lean and mean, more appreciative. Too much made him too fat. It had something to do with the law of diminishing marginal utility, about how the last increment of wealth was less appreciated than the first increment, even though the size of the increments were the same. The economics of Hershey bars.

He never understood dollar bills beyond the law of supply and demand, which covered all the crimes the world had ever known, which in turn covered the entire field of economics. He was on a random jag now, and the more he thought about it, the more he understood Amos. Amos Random was the name. The old man was contrary consistently, but just try to deal with the contrary consistently. Hugh should have known that Amos was blowing his stack too much at the idea of selling his land and that sooner or later he would come around and take on the bait. The trouble was that Amos was supply and demand at the same time, so what could you do?

Facing off with Perley wasn't a good Amos idea. Wrong time. Wrong way. You didn't blast your neighbor with an insult cannon, shelling him with "Genghis

152

Khan" and "Hitler" bombs. On the other hand, it might have been something to see.

He turned off the asphalt and drove into the woods on the gravel-sand-mud road that wound through the maples and pines. Past the Perley place, Past Benj Carver's. At Amos's, he turned into the long approach road, glorious Chelsea Pond to the right.

It's not me who's gumming it up, Hugh thought. But play it smooth, play it smooth. The old man is against the wall, and he's looking for an opening. Force Amos against a wall and you got a snarl going. Maybe Rita is right. That's the tactic, but whose?

Hugh always looked for Amos outside first. The trees, the land underfoot, the outdoors plain and simple were the man's habitat. If he wasn't there, he'd be in some outbuilding second. Not there, he'd be—last—in his house. So it was. Amos was futzing in the sugarhouse, and Rita was there, too.

He saw them through the open door, propped wide with a log. Rita saw him coming, waved, and led Amos outside.

"Too late to eat," Amos shouted, holding a plumber's wrench around a feed pipe to the evaporator.

"I don't eat pipe for dinner, Amos."

"Ha!" Rita burst out, laughing long and loud. "But *he* does! That's him all right. Ha!"

Amos jerked his thumb at her. "She'll laugh at anything so long as it's not funny."

Hugh stood grinning, looking at rough-and-ready Rita, tough sapling out to check the jungle onslaught of the world, and next to her, ambling Amos with his barbs that irritated the hell out of you. What a pair.

"You don't think he fed *me*, do you?" she said.

"I trained her years ago not to come at dinner time," Amos said to catch up. "It worked."

They dueled and jabbed until Hugh got them down to

business. "Now what's all this about Perley?" he asked, eyes on Amos, taking up where the telephone call left off. Then he switched to Rita. "Did he tell you about it?"

She nodded and rolled her eyes.

"First you want me to sell my LAND," Amos shouted. "Then you say no. You a walking pendulum?"

"I didn't say for you to sell your land. Just get the word out there."

"Well, I'm *going* to sell my land. Getting out of here. You told me I was going to get killed."

"I didn't say that."

"You saying I'm going deaf first?"

Hugh clamped his mouth and glanced at Rita.

"I'm going to sell my land to the closest Hitler around here and that's Perley. I told him so."

"Told him what?"

"I went up there and I said, 'PERLEY, you Genghis Khan Hitler, I never did like you, and Benj never did like you and your New Jersey spit-ball house, but before I sell you my land I'm telling you what I think of you."

"Judas, Amos."

"Where?"

Hugh grinned and shook his head. Rita was glancing at him first this time, grinning, too.

"Then I changed my mind," Amos said, shaking the pipe wrench and crimping his face like an old balloon.

"You changed your mind? Right there?"

"Where else?"

"Amos," Rita said, unable to hold back any longer, "that's the stupidest thing I've ever heard you do. Sell your land! You can't do it. You know what that creep will do to it. You're doing it because Ernie Carver thinks you *won't* do it."

"That toad-brained tulip bulb, he's a TRAITOR going out there to *Arizona*. ARIZONA! Next thing he'll go to TEXAS!"

154

"What do you mean, you changed your mind?" Hugh asked.

"I changed my mind. That's Greek? I took my mind and I changed it. It's my mind, you know."

"Yeah, we know that all right," Rita said.

"So what'd you tell Perley?"

"I told him, I changed my mind. I said, 'PERLEY, I just changed my mind. I'm looking at you and I ain't going to sell my land to you or nobody. I'm not a traitor.' That's what I said."

Hugh inhaled. "Amos, you're provoking the guy."

"Why'd you even go up there?" Rita said, charging in. She stepped closer; Amos stepped away. "How many times do we got to tell you. The man's a greed machine. He'll tell you anything, *do* anything, to get the land around here. Don't you see that? He's a creep. He's a monster in a business tie and he'll gobble up this land of yours if you give him half a chance. You're giving him that chance, Amos, and he'll take the rest of it and stuff it down our throats."

Amos turned and walked like a resolute bulldog into the sugarhouse. Rita followed him in, then Hugh.

"That's why we got to fight him, Amos," she pleaded, "fight him."

Amos clanked the pipe wrench and pipe into the empty bed of the evaporator he was cleaning. He picked up a hammer and whacked the wrench free. Then he took a rag and wiped the pipe clean.

Rita went to one side of the evaporator, Hugh to the other. Amos glowered at the rag as he rubbed nothing in particular.

"Well, what did Perley say about all this?" Hugh asked.

"Perley says he's been talking with Ernie *Carver*. He tells me that, right to my face. Right there in his spit-ball house, he tells me that. Ernie *Carver*. I said, 'Yeah, I

155

know. You flew him out here, paid his way.' He says, 'How'd you know that?' I said, 'I got my ways.' Didn't tell him about you."

Hugh shrugged.

"So what else?" Rita said. Her hands gripped the edge of the evaporator, holding up her body leaning toward Amos.

"We weren't talking daisies, you know."

"I know that, Amos," she said. "But what else? What'd he say?"

"I told you."

"What *else?*"

"You can tell a man's naked as a jaybird when you tell him something he thought was secret, you know," Amos said. "So I stood there and sort of smirked and grinned. You know what I mean. 'Course, anybody'd fly a Carver from ARIZONA, *pay* his way so's he can talk to him, got something wrong going. So I got him there."

"Thanks to Hugh, here," Rita said.

"I woulda smelled that Carver sooner or later."

"So what'd he say to that?" Rita asked, words flying fast. "What'd he do?"

"Just told you."

"What else? What else?"

Amos looked to Hugh for mock relief. "So he said something about his business was *his* business and he didn't like people snooping around *his* business. I said, 'Listen, PERLEY, this land is MY business and I'm looking to it. You just changed your mind, PERLEY,' I said to him. 'I ain't gonna sell my land to you.' Then he said it."

When Amos shuffled like a rhino on his feet, Rita couldn't hold back. "What?"

"He said Ernie Carver and him was making a deal on old Benj's land and that was it. Nothing I could do. It was Carver land and Ernie Carver was a CARVER. He

156

said when it was PERLEY land he'd do what he wanted to do with it."

Rita exploded her hands in front of her. "What'd I tell you?"

"So he's going to get the Carver land, right?" Hugh said.

"How do I know?" Amos said. "You believe somebody named PERLEY?"

"He's talking about condominiums," Rita said, pacing to the door and back. "He's dreaming of little clone houses all in a row and asphalting a whole development here. He's after shoreline, Hugh, I know it. He wants that lake, speedboats, and hot dog stands. It's all coming. It's his heaven, because he'll grab the millions and head out someplace else while we're still here fighting the asphalt and quickie burgers and wondering what happened and why we didn't do something when we had the chance. It's all there, I can see it, I'm telling you."

"Maybe," Hugh said.

"Condos," she said, "Perley loves condos because it jams people in one place so they can shove more money in his greed machine." She shook her head and clawed her fingers. "It's all there. That's his plan."

"So how'd you leave it?" Hugh asked Amos.

"We weren't talking daisies, you know."

"I know."

Amos looked at Rita. "Sure, he's thinking condominiums."

"Damn right."

"So that was it?" Hugh asked again.

"You think so?" Amos said, turning to Hugh, who shrugged. "Nope. He said something else." He shifted his eyes to Rita and Hugh, like figuring whether he should tell or not.

"What?" Rita said, hands pleading to get on with it.

"He said he'd get my land, too. Said it. I heard it with

my own ears. I said, 'PERLEY, I changed my mind, I ain't selling you nothing.' Then he says, 'I'll get it sooner or later. You know why?' he says. 'Cause, I got ways.' He said it: 'I got ways.' And then he says, 'Besides, you're an old, dying fart and when you blow out I'm grabbing your land.' Said that.''

"Hugh," Rita said, clutching his forearm, "we've got to fix that man. Get him out of here. We got to do something. He shouldn't be here. He should be back there in his trash-can city someplace."

"That ain't all," Amos said.

"What?"

Amos switched his glaring eyes back and forth from Rita to Hugh. "Said he was getting old Benj's land all right. He was working on it. Said Ernie CARVER told him he and his brother hate my guts 'cause I was a Reed and all that. But he got it twisted the wrong way. Then he said it."

"What?"

"He said I better sell him my land now or else."

"Or else what?" Rita said, leaning her eyes toward him.

When Amos looked to Hugh and said nothing, just stared, Hugh said, "What'd he say, Amos?"

"He said he'd level my grove tree by tree until I DID sell it to him."

"He said that?" Rita asked, eyes unwavering.

"I told you, didn't I?"

Rita twisted around in a circle, head up, fists clenched. "He told you that? That's a threat. That's criminal. We could have him prosecuted for that."

They fell silent, all three staring at the empty evaporator.

"It's hearsay," Hugh said at last. "He hasn't done anything like that."

"Not yet," Rita said.

"What'd he say exactly, Amos?"

"Told you. He looks at me and he says, 'I'll cut your trees down one by one 'til you sell out.' That's what he said."

"Did he say, 'to him?' Sell to him?"

"Sure he did."

"So what?" Rita said. "He'll do it, too. He's a hood, Hugh. He's trash on the land. He doesn't give a damn."

"It matters," Hugh said. Then to Amos: "Did he?"

"Sure, he did."

"You see?" Rita said at once. "It's a direct criminal threat. The man'll do anything to get Amos's land. He doesn't want the orchard, he wants the shorefront."

Hugh turned to Rita. "Amos goes up there and challenges him," he said. "Perley returns the compliment."

"I change my mind. That's a CHALLENGE?"

"I think we ought to tell the Chief and get him to bring in the troopers, get the attorney general in here," Rita said. "You don't wait around on something like this. Amos's orchard will end up cordwood if we don't get going on this. Perley's behind these killings. He's got to be."

"Rita," said Hugh, the supplicant, "nothing's happened." He turned to Amos. "Anything missing? Any trees down?"

"Perley touches one of my trees and PERLEY'S sweeping up house ashes," Amos said, picking up the pipe wrench and banging it against the inside of the evaporator.

"What about Ernie?" Rita asked.

"Don't talk to me about HIM," Amos shouted. "That toad bird ain't staying at Benj's 'cause he knows he can't sleep that close to me thinking what I'm *thinking* of that CARVER TRAITOR, him coming in here desecrating the place, sneaking in over at that Anderson place, PERLEY buying him off like that. 'Course, he's BUY-

ING him off like that. Anybody can buy off that two-bit ARIZONA cowboy hick traitor, going out there like that, coming back here *plaguing* me."

"Right," Rita said, fueling the fires, "he's doing that. He's—"

"Well," Hugh interrupted, "let's let it be for now, OK?"

"Be what?" Amos said.

Hugh grinned. "Just keep it cool for now."

"How can you?" Rita said.

They stared at the evaporator.

"I'll come by tomorrow," Hugh said.

"For dinner?" Amos asked.

Hugh laughed. Finally, Rita did, too.

"I don't serve dinner," Amos said, "Ain't no restaurant around here, you know. Besides, I'm going to eat at Janice's. Staying over there."

"Oh?" Rita said, grinning and nodding, "you're fixing dinner for her?"

Amos jabbed his thumb at her and looked at Hugh. Then he said, with the ambiguity dangling, "Never did know anything about women's work."

19

It is not difficult to deceive a deceiver.

—La Fontaine

THE NEXT MORNING Amos called Hugh and shouted into the phone, "You up yet?"

"What do you think, Amos? I got work to do."

"That's what I mean."

"Very funny."

"I want you to come up here tonight."

"I thought you were going to stay at Janice's."

"Changed my mind."

"You're changing your mind a lot these days, Amos. Why, what's on tonight?"

"Plenty." He paused to let the word have its reins.

"Well?"

"Just get up here tonight. I got something to show you. Something to do. So no dance parties tonight. Cancel 'em. There's going to be some stuff going on here."

Hugh waited, his curiosity perking his stance, cocking his head. "What?"

"Just be here. Only walk."

"Walk."

"Left, right, left, right. Only don't walk on the road. Go up the old tote road by the Jacobs's. You know it."

"Yes."

"Nobody'll see you."

"What's going on, Amos?"

"You'll see."

"What time?"

"Eat first."

Hugh laughed.

"What's so funny?"

"Nothing."

"Be here at 8:30."

"Where?"

"In the sugarhouse, where do you think? And don't *tell* anybody."

"If you say so."

"NOBODY."

"Right, Amos. Nobody. Now, what's the difference between now and then. Tell me what's going on."

"Nothing's going on. I'm talking to you."

Hugh laughed.

"I'm serious about this."

"I know you are, Amos, but what's the difference between telling me now and then?"

"Plenty."

"All right, OK. I'll be there."

"Walk. Up the tote road. And don't tell *nobody*. I got something to show you. You remember all that?"

"Right, Amos. In the sugarhouse at 8:30."

"Lot to remember all day for you, you know."

Hugh Quint did what he was told. He left an hour before his appointed time and walked up the Old King's Highway, relic of the British days when giant, virgin-white pine timbers were hauled to Portsmouth and then shipped across the ocean blue to Great Britain for making into ship masts. No masts, no empire.

At the Jacobs's place at the end of the asphalt turnoff, he walked onto a latter-day tote road, scarcely visible to a watchful eye, not at all to a lazy one. Car travel, dogs barking, yelling kids faded away as the abandoned road slanted down bouldered and beeched hills, leaving Lyme behind.

Hugh had to contend with fearless chirping chipmunks and chickadees that paralleled him to the ends of their territories before letting the next batch take up patrol. They kept him alert in the dark and detailed woods.

He hoped to God that Amos wasn't on another snarl or cooking up heat that could backfire. He should have forced it out of Amos, what he was up to, what the old cuss was lassoing him into. You didn't play clown cook in a kitchen of dynamite.

The tote road faded away. Half a century ago, maybe more, the loggers had their fill and went elsewhere. Hugh walked onto a ghost footpath that took over from the road. He followed it through the thickened woods, between gray mounds of primordial boulder, across a ravine, along the edge of a swamp.

When Chelsea Pond came into view, he followed the trail as it stayed discreetly in the trees and wound around a hugh bulge in the lake. Once over a long gradual rise, he saw Amos's napkin-neat sugar grove and the old Reed house rooted as if it had grown there forever.

The closer he stepped to the sugarhouse, the more he studied it. Where was the sound of hammering and banging inside, the cursing like a nun, only loud? Where was the commotion?

He knocked on the rough-hewn door. "Amos?"

No answer.

"Amos?" he said again as he unlatched the door and pushed it open. That was when Hugh Quint spun his wheels.

Ernie Carver and Amos Reed were standing at the evaporator, waiting and watching Hugh open the door. They wore the same hunched-head look on their faces they always did, and they stared at Hugh as Hugh stared at them, only their eyes were ready for it.

163

"You're late," Amos said. Then he marched forward, with Ernie Carver following right behind, and stepped toward the doorway.

Hugh reflexed out of the way. He was staring too much to think about it.

"Come on," Amos shouted at him and headed outside.

Hugh watched the two marching old rhinos as they tramped the ground with heavy boot and chugging arm. What the hell was going on?

He followed them on command, catching up to make a single-file squad of Amos in the relentless, plodding vanguard, Ernie Carver second, Hugh Quint the rear end. Through a military stand of pines and into the handsome maples they went, until Hugh couldn't keep down the bubble in his stew.

"Amos?" he called, "what's going on here?"

"Confusing, ain't it?"

"What're you doing here, Ernie?"

"Walking."

Hugh shook his head: Another Amos. "I'm serious."

"You serious, Ernie?" Amos called back, twisting his head and mouth over his shoulder, barking out his husky, heavy voice.

"I'm serious."

"Me, too."

So Hugh followed them through the woods, down a shallow dip in the terrain, and then up the long, gradual incline. The two old men stepped onward as if going downstairs, but then halfway up Amos slowed down to half pace. The angle of his head and back made it plain:: He was slowing down for Ernie Carver (it sure wasn't for Hugh) because he was remembering that Ernie was back from Out There in the desert someplace, which was where he probably got cancer in the first place. He wasn't going to point it all out, though.

At half pace, the three of them climbed the rest of the hill. "Getting winded, Hugh?" Amos called back.

"Naw," he answered, breathing hard.

Amos was taking them straight for the stone wall at the crest of the hill, the dividing line between Reed and Carver land, and he was heading for the high-point of the crest besides.

When they reached it, Amos straight away climbed over the wall, turned around, and waited for Ernie and Hugh to do the same.

"This is it," he said. "We stay here."

"Yep," Ernie said.

Amos stepped a pace to a flat-edged boulder in the wall, sat down, and leaned against it. Ernie did the same. Hugh shook his head and followed suit. All three sat looking at old Benj Carver's disarrayed sugar orchard.

Hugh let a couple minutes go. Then he said, "OK, Amos, what's this all about?"

"We wait for dark."

"Then what?"

"You'll see."

"Think he can see in the dark?" Ernie asked Amos.

"Probably lost it with all those light bulbs," Amos said, analyzing Hugh as if he were back home.

Hugh put his elbows on his knees and shook his head.

"It's worth it," Amos said, leaned his head against the granite, and intertwined his fingers on his stomach. He grew taut and mumbly, his sighs angry and hard. "Traitor," he muttered, but it wasn't directed to Ernie sitting there in earshot, and Ernie made no sign of application, as if the two of them had already discussed the word. No, Amos was simmering heat inside for somebody else, and his bullnecked crouch and snarling sighs were showing it.

They sat there until daylight faded. The trees kept

most of the stars out; the moon on the low rising edge slanted half-light through the branches and trunks, but not enough to walk easy by. It was an owl's night, and in the distance they hooted their whoos.

"How long we waiting here?" Hugh asked, lowering his voice, the stillness having its sway.

"Long enough," Amos hissed, giving the clue to keep it low.

"An hour?"

"Maybe six or seven," he said, glowering. Then Amos muttered, "Not right. Dirty business. Making me do this." He was fuming mad, squirming and hot.

Hugh stayed clear of him and let it go. He'd find out sooner or later. Ernie obviously already had come to terms with whatever was provoking Amos.

The wild came out as the moon slanted down its light. The owl kept hooting. Branches creaked from something. Field mice scampered like sewing machines. Some big scratchy feet sounded down the hill someplace.

"Porcupine," Ernie whispered.

The moon was three hours high or so, Hugh figured, when Amos leaned without a word to catch Ernie's attention. Ernie nodded. Amos looked at Hugh and put a crooked finger to his mouth.

The two old men twisted slowly around; Hugh followed suit. They peered over the edge of the clumpy rock wall to Amos's land.

Hugh was thinking he was being suckered by two old pros. What was he doing with them here? What were *they* doing together? Reed and Carver? Oil and water didn't mix; they clashed. Where was the clash?

The movement caught his eye. Upright. Stick figure in the darkness. The pillared, vertical trunks heightened the horizontal swing in the black distance.

They watched, mesmerized by the vague, enticing

flutter of motion against the wide spread of waiting, almost trapping, trees.

What Hugh couldn't decipher was the weirdness of the gait. It had a grotesque gangliness about it, limbs and angles where they shouldn't be, extra joints and outsized extensions. Then he realized what it was all about a fraction before Amos whispered, "Chainsaw."

Ernie nodded.

The outer part was a rifle. The silhouette of wide butt funneling to a point alternated swings with the chainsaw. Distance was the deceiver. The outlines were confusing, but deciphering "chainsaw" in the middle of the night led to "trespassing," which led to "crime" and "murder" and "rifle."

They strained their watch, studying the scene down the hill, following the murky figure as it stick-walked through the pale strips of moonlight, in and out the weave of shadow-black tree trunks. Their lungs moved and that was all.

Then the gangly walking shadow stopped. The owl hooted.

Hugh couldn't tell who it was. If didn't matter. He was fascinated by the gray-blackness of the scene, the subtlety of what was locking his attention. He wasn't ready to interfere. He was immersed in spying. He was waiting. Like Amos and Ernie. Which was just as fascinating. It was a loop.

He glanced at Amos. The old man was tight as a hook. Any tighter and sparks would be flying out his eyes. His face was scrunched in fury, deep furrows at his eyebrows, jaw clamped like a safe of TNT.

The silhouette moved again, this time changing direction, although it was too dark to tell how much. The distortion of a colorless world made it too uncertain.

Behind the safe rocks, they watched the mute black-

and-white screen. Then, when the spectre stopped again and this time set the chainsaw down and propped the rifle against a tree, Amos looked to Ernie and jerked his head. Ernie nodded.

Amos and Ernie led the way, two old, crouching turtles running on their bent legs on the Carver side of the stone wall so their footsteps wouldn't sound over the edge and down the Reed hill. Hugh followed crouching, too, unseen, unheard.

About fitty yards along the wall, they stopped and leveled their breaths, glancing at each other, serious and taut.

They crept to the wall and raised their heads to the top. The silhouette was closer, larger, but still painted night black and indecipherable. The difference was that they could hear the quick rustle of dampened noise, the clank of metal.

Hugh looked to Amos, who stared straight ahead and patted the air for patience and *no* noise.

When the chainsaw sputtered and boomed into action, the night woods burst into an ugly, shattering cacophony, as if night glass had shattered into a thousand shards. The loud, burring machine noise caught and held, ripping up the silence. Then, when the gnarring teeth cut into the base of a hard maple, the sound dipped on impact before regaining its momentum and went on gouging and tearing the life out of the tree.

The blatantness of igniting a cacophonous chainsaw in the middle of the night was sign enough. Nobody would do it on Amos Reed's land unless rampaging Amos was long gone, unless somebody thought that Amos was gone, that Amos was staying with his daughter Janice that night. The ratcheting shrill of the saw kept on with an impunity that wasn't going to last.

Amos looked to Ernie and, this time, Hugh. His eyes

were hot-tempered cold steel; he jerked his head: This was it.

The three of them climbed over the boulders. They kept their eyes on the tree-mangling noise, kept themselves crouched, kept tight.

Without a sign, they spread into a three-spoked fan, half circling the target.

The closer they got, the more Hugh deciphered the scene. He heard his boot crack a twig, but it didn't matter. The chainsawer was wearing ear-protectors against the roaring, spewing machine. He recognized the silhouette now, knew the thin, tough frame on the rugged, outraged woman.

It was over in a second, fast as murder.

They crept, catlike, up behind her. She was deaf to the world, except for that blaring, gnawing, destroying machine she hated.

Ernie was closest to the rifle. He made one last, careful step and grabbed it.

Rita caught the quick jerk of movement out the corner of her eye. She turned and quick-froze in absolute horror.

Hugh saw the panicked whites of her eyes. He stared at her until she broke her terror and saw Amos there, too.

The chainsaw roared on. When she turned it off, the silence was ugly.

20

Always do right. This will gratify some people, and astonish the rest.

—Mark Twain

CHIEF ATKINS SHUT the blue-and-white door on Rita in the back seat. He turned to the three men and pursed his lips. "Can't believe it," he said.

"You heard her," Amos growled, tight-faced.

"Heard enough."

"Yeah."

The Chief nodded and then shook his head. "I've known her a long time, long time, but I guess the district attorney's office will be talking with her."

"Yeah, well, I *ain't* talking with her," Amos said. "Don't give nothing to NOBODY." He looked away from them to the ground.

Hugh caught the Chief's brief look of bewilderment that good ol' Rita could end up like this. "You'll need us later,' he said, letting him know that Hugh knew this wasn't the Chief's usual stuff.

"Yeah," Atkins said, closing it all off, looking at each of them, nodding finally to silent Ernie. He got into the blue-and-white and slammed the door.

Rita looked through the back side-window at Amos. She was an exhausted, drained, caught woman. A killer. Her eyes sought absolution from the old man, but the refusing old man hunched his betrayed soul to the ground.

The Chief drove off without the blue lights whirling or sirens whining because, well, it was just Rita.

When the Chief had driven far enough away for Rita not to see, Amos turned and looked out the corner of his eye at the car, and sniffed.

Amos and Ernie and Hugh went into the sugarhouse and sort of hung around, fiddling with the pipes and bottles, the bow saw hanging on the wall. They didn't say anything until Amos finally pulled out a drawer, popped the cork on a Scotch bottle, and asked, "Who wants one?"

"What's that doing in there?" Hugh asked.

"Hiding from women."

Ernie laughed. Then Hugh, and Amos, who poured three rounds in miniature plastic glasses he used to test syrup.

"What the hell are you two doing?" Hugh said. "What happened to the Reeds and Carvers? You suckered me, Amos."

"ME?"

"You talking to a Carver."

Ernie laughed. "He called me about it."

"Voice never the same," Amos said, "wandering around out there in the DESERT."

"And a *Carver* talking back," Hugh said, shaking his head. "I don't know. Really suckered."

"I flew back," Ernie said. "We figured it this way. I pay the fare here, Amos pays me to go back there. I know he's figuring that once I'm here I won't go back. So he comes out ahead. Reeds are like that."

Hugh held up his hands. "Wait a minute," he said. "You mean Perley never flew you back here?"

Ernie and Amos grinned at each other.

"Perley never cooked up this scheme?"

"PERLEY'S a hole in a doughnut," Amos shouted. "You think he knows something?"

Ernie shook his head and smiled.

"Your mistake, great Hugh," Amos shouted, "was you never checked it with PERLEY. 'Course, I knew you wouldn't want to go over there talking with that tin bucket. So what I said goes. Only you weren't supposed to stumble on Ernie here."

"I had to plant some seeds fast," Ernie said.

"They grew, too!" Amos shouted, and bellowed out a laugh.

"Yeah, yeah," Hugh said.

"Sprouting all *over* the place," Amos said, laughing and giggling. "Easy stuff when you got good soil to till."

"Yeah, sure," Hugh said. "What about Rita?"

"Don't talk to me about her," Amos shouted with lightning-quick rage. He sliced his hand through the air to guillotine her away.

"Come on, Amos," Hugh said.

"Perley!" he said to change the subject. "All this don't cut that cigar butt free and clear, you know. He's still lusting after my land, and Ernie's here, too, and who says he ain't maneuvering and scheming RIGHT NOW to get it. There are other ways of killing things, you know."

"I know you're angry about Rita," Hugh persisted.

Amos shot him a hot, puckered look. "Betrayed me, that's what she did. Friends don't kill neighbors. Went and did what I don't do. Friends don't do what you don't do." He grabbed a wrench and smashed the flat side against the evaporator, jarring the sugarhouse silence.

"They don't," Ernie said.

Amos downed the Scotch in a gulp and let Hugh and Ernie watch him fill the cup again. He shifted back and forth on his feet. "Why did she go and do that?" he said, the old voice down and almost out. He shook his head. "Makes me sorrowful."

"But you knew," Hugh said.

"Sure, I knew," Amos said, shuffling. "Knew she was right about PERLEY getting after the land here, too, *probably* right. Thieving know-nothing. But I know something or two, and I got to suspecting her. Going over the edge like that, mad as a wet hen all the time and getting OBSESSED with this place and that PERLEY, and then she's always away and then too close when them shots come through the window. *She* did it. You'll get to know women, Hugh, you got time."

"So," Ernie said, "we got together and fixed it up. Amos, he never told Perley anything like he was going to sell his land. He told *you*."

"Yeah, I told you," Amos said and laughed. "But then you was coming in here and telling *me* about it, getting me to say it. That was OUR idea you hit on, and that got me real nettled, but with you racing in here like that we had to race faster. Old and grumped don't mean stupid and dumb, you know."

"Then Rita showed up," Hugh said, picturing her tossing logs into the firebox under the evaporator, tossing them like pick-up sticks. She could wrap tubing around Davy Tefler's neck all right, and stab Bill Kanin in the back with one plunge. Shove Benj into the boiling sap. She knew the woods like the palm of her hand, knew the caves at Webster's Rocks.

"Yeah," Amos interrupted, "she was here so I told you PERLEY told me he was going to cut down my trees one by one if I didn't sell to him. She heard it all right. Flushed her out. Then I told you I was going to Janice's, going to stay there, staying there overnight, wouldn't be here. She heard that, too. Ha! She planned it right then— cut down one of my babies and blame it on PERLEY."

Hugh grinned and nodded.

"Yeah, Rita," Amos said, shaking his head, "don't like netting her like that, but don't like her killing and setting it up, killing good ol' Benj like that. I'm missing him, you know." He put his hand on Ernie's shoulder, but not too long. He got back to shouting. "So I got to *thinking*."

"What I don't get," Hugh said, "is how you got the gumption to get Ernie in on this."

"WHAT?" Amos shouted, his face turning into a neck-back, eye-popping angle of disbelief. "You don't know? You joking me?"

Hugh spread his hands.

"Can you believe this?" Amos said to Ernie.

Ernie shrugged.

"We're talking *choices* here," Amos shouted. "Sure PERLEY'S after my land. He's after Benj and Ernie's. Rita is right about that, but PERLEY is from New JERSEY. NEW JERSEY! That's right next to New YORRRKKK! 'Course, I called Ernie, what do you think? They believe trees grow in magazines down there. You want me to like living next to someone like that? Next to THAT!"

Nothing thinned a neighbor's blood like a good feud between old families over land, and nothing thickened it like a greedy stranger moving in. Hugh saw it plain enough. Amos could hate Benj and Ernie because the Reeds hated the Carvers and always had, and vice versa, but when someone like Henry Perley moved in, that was a different story. Old-timers could coagulate against these interloping bulldozers faster than a fall freeze. Amos and Ernie would rather shake hands any day of the week than sign with Perley. It was the only thing in the world to get Ernie Carver back from Arizona. He was dying of cancer maybe, but he was always dying to give it to somebody like Henry Perley. Any Carver would.

It was Rita that Hugh had to talk about. He called Proctor Hammond.

"Speak."

"Quint."

"Oh."

"You're glad to hear from me, I see."

"Thrilled. I thought some obit writer was calling me today about you, but you're still alive up there in that killer jungle. You're all right, I take it."

"I got suckered a couple times, got shot at a couple times."

"I got shot a couple times. Diphtheria, tetanus."

Hugh smiled into the phone. "Rita Dinsmore," he said and let the rest fill in.

"Yeah, you told me about her," Proctor said in his dissecting tone.

"Can't really figure it, though."

"I can," Proctor interrupted, and off he went. "She got fed up. She fought the good fight with the right rules for twenty years and she still saw the world being demolished, and she's right. So she cracked and joined the terrorists. If you can't trap the bulldozers, you blame it on them. That's what she did. She set it up to blame what's-his-name?"

"Henry Perley."

"Henry Perley. She had to make it look bad. So she killed 'em to blame him. Say it's crude, but crude's the truth. She went flying, she went kill crazy, bananas, turned into a gorilla just like half the world out there, Quint, only you think it's an aberration but it's standard procedure down here in this asphalt Amazon. You up there in the pretty trees don't know what civilization is. You think it's furry little creatures digging for acorns. You think this Rita what's-her-name is a cute little thing, only she happened to get a touch of virus. But she got cancer of the Ten Commandments instead and figured to beat the system by using the same tactics the system used to beat her—lies, deception, sabotage, murder, all of it. More standard procedure. Nothing new about it, that's the way it works, and Rita came to realize that. She knew she was up against the barbed wire system and this Henry Perley was coming in to stake his post. All she was doing was trying to save some land, a few measly trees, keep that puddle up there from turning into another motorboat cesspool, and she couldn't do it with just little bushy-tailed creatures on her side. She got obsessed with winning something in her life."

"Obsessed?"

"Obsessed, obsessed," Proctor sped into the phone, "she got carried away with herself, couldn't stop herself. She had to win one, so it came to her to frame a big one on The System and that was Henry Perley and his chrome-plated bulldozers. So she killed one and then another one and then another one. She couldn't stop, kept right on, building up the arrows at Perley, surrounding him with pointing fingers. She was obsessed, all right."

"Anybody can get obsessed."

"Anybody could, and once people get going on something they start gnawing and clawing at the same old wall, same old thing, only more of it, can't stop."

"You obsessed, Proctor?"

"Who's obsessed? What're you talking about? Who's obsessed?"

176